SO THE ARROW FLIES

A solo performance piece
conceived, written and performed
by

Esther K. Chae

NoPassport Press
Dreaming the Americas Series

Developed at the Mark Taper Forum Theatre Solo
Performance Workshop, Winter 2005

Archived at Library of Congress, Asian American
Performing Arts Series 2012

Performance time approximately 85 min

Book design and typography by Seiyoung Park
Cover art by Piyanari Lefebvre
Art direction by Boyoung Lee

NoPassport Press, www.nopassport.org
ISBN: 978-1-312-27592-8

For Dr. Hi-kyung Chae and Mrs. Inja Chae.

Thank you Umma and Appa for giving me life,
good sense and stories to share.

CONTENTS

FOREWORD

By David Henry Hwang

It's become expected, perhaps even a cliché, for literary works by Asian Americans to explore issues of identity. Certainly, "Who am I?" is a universal human inquiry, relevant across time and geographical distance. The tendency of Asian American authors (including myself) to feature this question, however, arguably dovetails with how we are perceived as "perpetual foreigners." One's forebears may have arrived in America many generations ago, but we still might hear, "You speak such good English!" Similarly, virtually every Asian American has been asked the loaded question, "Where are you from?" followed by "No, I mean, where are you really from?" Our experiences in this country leave us acutely sensitive to the slippery boundaries of identity. I sometimes ask myself, "Is there a new way to write an identity play?"

Happily, Esther K. Chae has created one of the freshest, most far-reaching, and profound explorations of this issue in years. I first met Esther as a talented and whip-smart actor in the company of my play, YELLOW FACE. She showed me an early draft of a solo performance piece she had written, which immediately thrilled and excited me. Centering on the interrogation of a possible North Korean double agent named Park, by a Korean American FBI agent also named Park, the characters in SO THE ARROW FLIES search for their identities while simultaneously trying to conceal them. That the accused spy was once a well-known North Korean actress whose features have been altered by multiple plastic surgeries, further complicates the thorny relationship between the interior and exterior selves. This play's multiple and interconnected storylines go even further, to explore how societies and governments seek to control their own dramatic narratives and images, within their own borders and to the world. Add to this the theatrical conventions of a one-person show, with Esther brilliantly transforming to portray four major characters by simply turning on a chair, and you have a piece whose form perfectly expresses its content.

The relationship between America and Korea has been fraught for over fifty years, and Esther captures the deconstructed, post-modern reality in which these nations now interact. This often-surreal dynamic also mirrors the complicated relationship between her play's mothers and daughters. SO THE ARROW FLIES manages the amazing feat of juggling all these strands of investigation, with clarity, intellectual rigor, and a big heart. Born in Oregon and raised in South Korea, Esther has created an important work which speaks not only to Asian and Asian American identity, not only to the U.S.-Korea relationship, but extends to international relations and the constantly-transforming nature of information itself in our current digitized age.

Is there a new way to write an identity play? Esther K. Chae answers this question with a resounding yes, through this dazzlingly ambitious play, which explores nothing less than the identity of our world today.

– David Henry Hwang
  Brooklyn, NY

SO THE ARROW FLIES

by Esther K. Chae

Photo credit: Junghoon Pi

Production History:

2012	Library of Congress, Performing Arts Playwright Series, Washington D.C., USA
	Arts Council of Korea, Seoul, Korea
	Wellesley College, Wellesley, USA
2010	October Nights Theater Festival, Imola, Italy
2010	University of Michigan, Ann Arbor, USA
2010	Sejong Society, American University, Washington D.C., USA
2010	Bennett Media Studio, New York, USA
2010	Cherrylane Theater, New York, USA
2009	Willdish Theater, Eugene (OR), USA
2009	CUNY's Martin Segal Theater, New York, USA
	NYU's Tuesday Night Forum Series, New York, USA
2009	Boston Court Perfomring Arts Center's ARTTalk Series, Pasdena, USA
2009	TED (Technology, Entertainment and Design) Conference, Long Beach, USA
2008	Ars Nova Theater Festival, New York, USA

2008	World Women's Forum, Seoul, Korea
2008	Edinburgh Fringe Festival, Edinburgh, Scotland
2008	David Henry Hwang Theater, Los Angeles, USA
2007	Manhattan Theater Source, Estrogenius Festival, New York, USA
2007	Armory Center, Pasadena, USA
2005	Mark Taper Forum Solo Workshop, Los Angeles, USA

Characters:

CATHERINE PARK, alleged North Korean spy, 30s

FBI AGENT JI-YOUNG PARK, Korean-American FBI Agent, 20s

MINA WHITE, Catherine's American-born hapa daughter, 12

MRS. PARK, Agent Park's immigrant mother, 60s

<u>Time:</u> Now

<u>Place:</u> Mrs. Park's Living Room, FBI Interrogation Room, FBI Office, Solitary Confinement Cell, Foreign Detainment Camp, Netherworld

Photo credit: Asa Mathat, Jared Asato, Corky Lee

Editor's Note:

This play was written as a vehicle for female actors of Asian descent. But, for educational purposes only, if students choose to perform monologues or scenes from the play as an exercise, gender, race and some references may be bent and re-imagined. For example, So the Arrow Flies was presented at the "October Nights Festival" in Italy and followed up with a master-class workshop. The Italian students in this particular workshop were both male and female of diverse ages and backgrounds. They performed varying roles as *Italians* (not as Koreans or Korean-Americans) from the play. The integrity of the characters and their relationship to one another remained intact, though Mrs. Park became *Mrs. Grandi*, an Italian mother worried about her Italian-American *son* working for the FBI.

On stage are a desk and a rolling black office chair that swivels. On the desk are a tape recorder, one FBI file, one pen and a glass of water.

SCENE 1: MRS. PARK / LIVING ROOM

MRS. PARK: *(off stage, in Korean) Okay, Jiyoung. I got it~**

Mrs. Park, Korean immigrant in her 60s, enters. She has a cardigan draped around her shoulders.

MRS. PARK *(in a Korean accent)*: Hello! Hi~ So sorry to keep you waiting, but my daughter Ji-young just called, and she can not join us for dinner tonight. She works very hard nowadays, even on weekends, because she has a very important case about a North Korean spy. Oh, I didn't tell you? My daughter is an FBI agent. Federal Bureau Investigation agent! I like to say that, sounds ve~ry cool.

My Ewha University alumni friends are scared of Ji-

* (Pronunciation) Geu-rae, Jiyoung-ah. Alat-da~ (Korean) 그래, 지영아. 알았다~

13

young. But that day she was in a hurry, so she just came down the staircase without her jacket on. And they saw the gun strapped around her. They said, "Uh-muh-na, she carries around a gun"? So I said, "She's a FBI agent, what does she carry around – banana"?

(sits in chair) I don't know what they are more scared of: that Ji-young carries around a gun, or that she works mostly with white Americans, or that she is not married or because they think she is gay, or because she has stupid horrible chestnut haircut! I think it's stupid short chestnut haircut. I keep telling her, "Look at all those women on CSI TV shows – they have nice hair!' But she doesn't listen to me. But I understand. She's very pretty you know. She can be very distracting to men, so she has to dull and mute herself. You know what I mean?

But most importantly, my daughter has to be inconspicuous because she put some bad villains into jail. And sometimes the villains come back out and hunt the agent down. In her desk, Ji-young has a photocopy of all the villains' faces who are now released from jail. She looks at it often to recognize them, just in case they come back after her. *(hushed)* So after I saw this on her desk, I secretly went into her room to make a photocopy of the photocopy. So, I too can study very carefully each face – what kind of eye color, how high the nose is, how sharp their chin is.

I see everything, I have noon-chi. *Noon-chi*. Ha. Too bad English doesn't have this word. It means, "eye-sense." *(points at her eyes)* Looking around and know what is going on. I have hyper awareness. So if I see those villains from the photocopy, I can report to police or call my daughter or distract them or do something. So I can be undercover agent for my daughter! You laugh now, but you are too young to understand. That is how a Umma's heart is. That is what I will do for my daughter.

Mrs. Parks shrugs her cardigan off onto the chair's back. Seated, she turns the chair upstage. Then she slowly gets up, transforming into Agent Park.

SCENE 2: FBI AGENT JI-YOUNG PARK / FBI INTERROGATION ROOM

*FBI Agent Park, Korean American woman in her late 20s with a slight Southern drawl. She turns on a tape recorder of a woman speaking to a man in North Korean dialect. *

Recording in Korean.

Comrade Song: *Nicely done, Comrade Park.*

Comrade Park: *Not at all, sir.*

Comrade Song: *The confidential information you provided us was delivered directly to the superior office.*

Comrade Park: *I see.*

Comrade Song: *We will be in touch soon, Black Butterfly.*

Comrade Park: *Yes, sir.*

Agent Park turns the tape recorder off.

---

* (Pronunciation) Park dong-mu, soo-go mahn-aht-seup-neh-da. (Korean) 박동무 수고 많았습네다.

(Pronunciation) Ah-nib-neh-da. (Korean) 아닙네다.

(Pronunciation) Dong-mu-ga joon bee-mil jung-bo-neun bah-ro sahng-boo gi-gwahn-eh bo-go het-seup-nee-da. (Korean) 동무가 준 비밀정보는 바로 상부기관에 보고했습네다.

(Pronunciation) Al-at seup-neh-da. (Korean) 알았습네다.

(Pronunciation) Goht gum-eun na-bee-eh-geh yul-rahk deul-ee-get-sup-neh-da. (Korean) 곧 검은나비에게 연락드리겠습네다.

(Pronunciation) Neh. (Korean) 네.

AGENT PARK: Even though the majority of this tape recording is a North Korean man speaking, I think we can come to the conclusion that this is your voice, Mrs. White.

Agent Park addresses the chair ("Catherine").

The Washington office intercepted this conversation June 12th of last year while you were in Seoul. I listened to all the phone calls you made trying to find out where your parties with President Kim were being held at. And phone calls to flower shops about sending bouquets to all your high powered friends and what not. And we usually don't track or bug our informants phone calls. So what was extraordinarily startling and confusing to me was that you were speaking to a *North* Korean man.

Now why would you be doing that? And who is this "Comrade Song" who so fondly refers back to you as "Comrade Park"?

(beat) For the purpose of this investigation you need to speak in plain American English, Mrs. White.

(goes to file) Let's look at all your different names, Mrs. White. Born Park Seung-hee 1967 in Najin, North Korea. Used same name in China but then in South Korea changed to Park Hekyung. Maiden name in the US was anglicized and listed with INS as Catherine Park. Park gets inverted since Koreans put their last names, first. And as we heard on tape you're referred to as "Comrade Park" also known as code name Black Butterfly. And of course, Catherine White that you kept after your divorce. Jesus, how many names are that, five? *(counts names)* I'm sorry, six. *(beat)* And to think you and I actually have the same family name Park...

Agent Park examines Catherine's face closely. Then from her FBI folder, she takes a black and white photo of Catherine that is different from her current face. Agent Park shows it to Catherine. In the photo, Catherine is wearing a North Korean uniform with a hat. Projection of the same photo up on the back wall or screen.

Do you have as many different faces as your names, Mrs. White? I got this photo of you when you were part of the People's National Theater as a "No. 1 Actor". That's right, I found out you used to be an actress in Pyungyang.

Shows photo offstage as if through FBI interrogation window.

Now, guys, how the heck did ya'll miss this…

Alrighty, let's start from your plastic surgeries.

Agent Park slowly sits into the chair and transforms into Catherine as the chair swivels around to face the audience.

SCENE 3: NORTH KOREAN SPY CATHERINE / FBI INTERROGATION ROOM

Catherine, an alleged North Korean spy in her late 30s, sits handcuffed and cross-legged with the previous photo in her hand. Speaks poised Standard American and both South and North Korean dialects.

CATHERINE: *(in Korean) Wow, I'm so impressed. You did a lot of homework. So where in heaven's name did you find that photo? Can we talk after I've had some water?**

---

* (Pronunciation) Eh mahni ssuht-neh. Ah-nee ee-gun ddoh uh-

(in English) Fine. I'll speak in English if you won't give me any water otherwise. Even though I know you understand both my North and South Korean, Agent Park. *(scans Agent Park up and down)* A young female Korean-American FBI agent... Very interesting. We might even be related, Agent Park.

Catherine refers to the black and white photo in her hand.

I really did look like Kim Jungsook, didn't I? *When did I have my plastic surgeries? Which one? My face changed more times than you can count on your...teeth.*

Everyone said that I was a spit and image of Kim Jung-il's mother, Kim Jungsook. But still, if I were really going to portray the mother of the nation in propaganda movies, I couldn't just look like her. I had to *be* her. I mean I was anointed to be one of the prestigious *ilho baewoo*, The No. 1 Actors of the Democratic People's Republic of Korea.

Catherine puts the photo on her lap. She indicates areas

---

dee-suh cha-jaht-suh, geu-reh? Juh-gee mool john mah-shi-go yeh-gi-ha-ja-goo. Mwuh? (Korean) 애 많이 썼네. 아니 이건 또 어디서 찾았어, 그래? 저기 우리 물 좀 마시고 애기하자구. 뭐?

fixed on her face.

Dr. Zielbauer in Munich said my eye shape and ear size were identical to Kim Jung-il's mother's. But he had to raise my nose 1.5 mm higher so my nostrils would be slimmer. Cheekbone injections. Chin sharper. Chest smaller. And, of course, the most important part. My vocal cords.

Catherine emphatically sings North Korean propaganda song "The Red Flag" with hand gestures.

CATHERINE: *(in Korean) Raise the red flag high and mighty. I shall swear under it!**

(in English) It was amazing. I was only 17 when I portrayed the dear leader's young mother in the movie "The Red Sun Continues to Shine". Fevered, passionate performances, mass games with my face plastered all over the stadium, expensive food and wine imported from Russia and Europe. Everyone loved us, the No. 1 Actors. They had to. It was their

---

* (Pronunciation) Noh-pee deu-ruh-rah, bool-geun git-bah-reul. Geu mit-eh-suh gut-geh meng-she-heh! (Korean) 높이 들어라 붉은 깃발을. 그 밑에서 굳게 맹세해!

obligation.

Catherine picks up the photos from her lap.

One day, you're the mother of the nation. Then the next, you're a refugee being hunted by that very nation you served. Ha! Life. Undulates very very oddly. Don't you think, Agent Park?

Catherine throws the photo to the ground.

So now. Tell me what you did with my daughter Mina.

SCENE 4: AGENT PARK / FBI INTERROGATION ROOM

Agent Park picks the black and white photo off the ground. She walks over to the FBI desk and opens her FBI file.

AGENT PARK: Your daughter Mina's safe. They're just asking her questions, standard procedures. In the meanwhile, let's get the following details out of the way first.

As Agent Park reviews her notes, projection of KIM family tree on the back wall or screen.

1994, once dictator number one Kim Il-sung dies, the regime changes over to his son Kim Jung-il. Then the mother of the nation, no, you, the actress portraying the mother of the nation, is ousted. Because dictator number two Kim Jung-il needs to clean house and start his own crazy legacy. And now he's dead and his pudgy son Kim Jung-eun is the next 'supreme leader' of North Korea. Unbelievable...

1994, that same year, you're exiled to the border of China and North Korea, to work as a surveillance manager and you flee. First into mainland China where you bust up your face again. So people wouldn't recognize your actress face as Kim Jungsook.

Agent Park takes out the previous black and white photo and another second colored photo, which also represents Catherine's previous face.

Too bad, you used to be really pretty. The Chinese doctor did a really good job making you look ugly.

Comes back to desk and puts both photos into the FBI file.

Then you escape to Mongolia and finally you succeed in getting into the Korean Embassy- and you are sent to Seoul. The South Korean newspaper here quotes, "Even the mother of the nation could not endure the torturous and impoverished life in North Korea." And this perks up the South Korean National Intelligence Service and they ask you to work for them. Is all of this correct?

Agent Park takes the glass of water from the desk and takes a long sip.

Agent Dakota was found dead two days ago. Right on the heels of Kim Jung-il's death. I find that very odd. You have any idea why?

Agent Park immediately transforms into Mina.

SCENE 5: MINA / SOLITARY CONFINEMENT

Mina, a 12-year-old, half-Korean, half-Caucasian American daughter to Catherine. She hollers a warrior cry from behind the chair, then jumps out and aims her arrows to different parts of the theater, as if reenacting a battle. She makes sounds of arrows flying as she shoots them, "pyoong~ pyoong~ pyoong!"

Suddenly, Mina is hit by imaginary arrows. The last one hits her heart. She staggers, then plunks into the chair and as she 'dies'...

MINA: Ha...ha..martia...

Mina goes limp in the chair. Beat. She wakes, adjusts her pig tails, then starts talking to the audience as if they were her 'imaginary best friend.'

So that's what I did, Joss! For our Greek tragedy homework! And of course Mrs. Cooper was like totally blown away by my presentation and gave me an "A+". Cuz nobody said that our Greek tragedy presentation couldn't be a theatrical one. Hello? So after I die, cuz the arrows hit me all over my body, I explain Aristotle's writing in the Poetics about hamartia. Ha-mar-*tia*, on the third syllable. Do you know what that means? Hamartia literally means "missing the mark" in archery but in Greek tragedy means, like, the hero's tragic flaw. Cuz they totally miss the point and that becomes their fatal error. And it's usually becuz they have too much hubris. You know what that means, right? Hubris is like, a lot of pride. Like you think you can do anything and that you can mess with everything. And if you have too much hubris, you basically become a dickhead. Like Michael Limbaugh.* He thinks he's so cool cuz he's dad's like a congressman or whatever but everyone in our class hates him cuz he's such a *D-I-C-K*. *(performs 'DICK' dance)* Even the teachers hate him. You so know it's true.

As Mina walks towards the desk, she transforms into Agent Park. After reading a memo on her desk, Agent Park grabs her file, goes around the outside of the desk and comes downstage center, stepping into her superior's office.

SCENE 6: AGENT PARK / FBI OFFICE

AGENT PARK: Yes, sir. She was ordered by us to give some information to North Korea under the code name Black Butterfly. But she was not supposed to

---

* Or any other current rabid Republican's last name.

hand over all those classified documents. I mean, it has all the scientists' names, their faces and which nuclear program they're working on. She also leaked photos from Agent Dakota's 60ᵗʰ birthday party, at which key senior FBI agents were present, including you, Sir. If you remember, Catherine's daughter Mina was taking photos. So it just looked liked an innocent kid was taking family pictures.

I do think Catherine being Agent Dakota's lover is the main reason why North Korea took him out. I'm not sure the order was under this new regime, though. They couldn't have moved that fast... Sir, has Catherine's daughter been released to go back home? Really? But there's a law against interrogating a minor, we could get into serious trouble. I know we're under time pressure sir, but I'm the only one combing through all the tapes. There's over 200 hours from Seoul, Pyungyang and DC.

The CIA? What do those clowns want?

Agent Park returns back to the desk, and drops her folder on it. As she grabs the cardigan from the chair's back and puts it over her shoulders, she transforms into Mrs. Park.

SCENE 7: MRS. PARK / LIVING ROOM

MRS. PARK: I am so proud of my daughter Ji-young. She is one of the youngest women to work for the FBI agency. Can you imagine, my daughter working for the American government? You are only truly integrated as an immigrant when you are representing your adopted country *verbally*. I know. I used to be a linguist professor in Korea. That is when your immigrant community has arrived.

Not scientist or engineer or doctor but more like – defense lawyer. You have to talk talk talk and make a good argument to win a case. Or actor. No, not playing some dumb delivery boy but when you play some heart-breaking beautiful character like, like ee-reum-ee muh-duh-ra…* Oh, Joan Chen! She was so good in that movie, The Last Emperor. I don't know how she always knows my heart. She's Chinese and not Korean, but that's OK.

Or FBI agent. Because you have to talk to all kinds of people and give them confidence that you are representing the United States, so they will give you

---

* What was her name… (Korean) 이름이 뭐더라…

vital information. If you have accent and don't act American, then you can not become FBI agent. I mean my daughter Ji-young has kind of strange southern accent because we lived in Georgia. But she still sounds American, you know what I mean?

(sits down in chair) Oh actually, I have another funny accent story. When Ji-young was at FBI Academy in Quantico, she had Fire Arms Instructor who was also Korean. And his English was kind of bad and it got worse when he got excited. So one day the students are doing shooting target exercise and the fake bodies are coming towards the students and Ji-young got scared and she froze when she was suppose to shoot. So the Korean instructor screams, "Ji-young what are you doing, *throw your gun!*" So Ji-young got very confused and took out her gun out and threw it at the target!!! No, no he meant "draw your gun, *draw!*" Silly Ji-young, she still should have known. Who throws a gun?

I know I also have an accent, but actually I am fluent in English. I even write poetry in English and probably know English better than most American people. But they don't know. They see me and say,

"Oh, she's so cute, she's so round, she's so funny, she has funny accent." And they think everything I say is stultiloquy. Foolish babbling, stultiloquy. You didn't know that word, did you?

(looks at her wrist watch) Ok, enough talking, we don't have to wait for Ji-young. Let's just go have dinner.

Mrs. Park immediately turns into Mina as she pushes herself upstage in the chair and shrugs her cardigan off onto the back of the chair.

SCENE 8: MINA / SOLITARY CONFINEMENT

MINA: I'm so hungry! They should at least give me some food… Pizza would be nice.

Mina anxiously peers out 'the prison door' downstage, then walks around her cell. She addresses her 'imaginary friend' again.

Yeah, my Mom's home but *(making something up)* she's not feeling good, she's in bed. And you know my Mom don't cook like your Mom. I know, like I'm the only kid that has an Asian Mom that don't cook, what's up with that.

Sits in chair, turned backwards.

You know what's so funny, though? My Mom's a total bad ass, like she didn't take any shit from my Dad when they were getting a divorce or she'll out talk anyone if they're disrespectful to her and stuff. But she's always telling me that I have to look out for her. That I'm her warrior that protects her. Cuz I guess she knows I've got her back and I'm not going to let anyone mess with her. Cuz... I understand. I understand! She's like a high powered, important executive ambassador working for world peace. And, and it's like a dangerous job, you know? And people don't like women, women of color being so smart and awesome. It's threatening. That's what Oprah said. And that's my mom. And that's you and me when we grow up.

Standing up from chair.

Hello, of course I'm part of the movement! just cuz I'm half Korean and half white don't mean I'm not down with the cause. Don't you know that flava and color always trumps over *nothingness*?

I know, my name is Mina White. *(sits back in chair)* So stupid and totally against my identity. I'm totally changing my name to Mina Park when I'm legally 18. You probably didn't know, but my name Mina just sounds anglo, but actually in Korean it has, like, a totally deep meaning. My Mom told me that if you write 미(mi)나(na) –

Mina writes the Korean characters in the air. Simultaneous animated projection is seen on the back wall in Korean and Chinese characters.*

– it means "pretty and beautiful" in Chinese. Isn't that cool? Huh, I don't know why it's a Korean name and has a Chinese meaning… Cuz we're not Chinese. I'll have to ask my mom when she wakes up. But not right now, she's finally home from her international travels, so I need her to rest.

Mina closes her eyes as if resting then transforms right into

---

* (Korean) 미나 (Chinese) 美娜

Catherine.

SCENE 9: CATHERINE / FBI INTERROGATION ROOM

CATHERINE: Have you ever been hungry, Agent Park? I mean really famished. From royalty to surveillance manger eating rationed food. I had no idea people were living like this. It got worse with that unprecedented famine that hit North Korea.

He's the reason I am still alive. My North Korean husband that the party chose for me when I was a No. 1 Actor was thankfully a nice man. He swam across the icy Dooman River to warn me to flee. Apparently I was being accused of trafficking with South Koreans. But North Korea exiled me to the border and I was dealing with the Chinese, not South Koreans. What were they accusing me for? Something was wrong, I mean I was a member of the No. 1 Actors, I portrayed our dear leader Kim Jung-il's mother, I had done nothing wrong against our country. But I had to flee further into mainland China and I waited. And waited. But I never heard from my husband that I should come back home. *(beat)* Sure, I can give you his name but they probably killed him off so…

When I first came to America I only watched soap operas – Guiding Light, General Hospital. This concept of who you choose to love, who you decide to marry. I love you, I love him, "I, I, I." No *we*, all *me*. So I tried this concept out on my ex-husband Frank White and it worked! I mean, I married him mostly for my US citizenship. But we did have a child together. So, it lasted while it did.

(beat) She's so smart, my daughter Mina. Articulate, vivacious, almost as tall as I am and she's only 12 years old. She doesn't know anything. You really still don't know where she's been taken?

You've clearly never been in love, Agent Park, have you? It might be a little difficult for you. I mean you act as if you're a man – short shuffled hair, deep voice with that *strange accent*. I don't think men find that attractive. Do your FBI colleagues really take you more seriously just because a small Asian woman is pretending to be like a white man? If anything Agent

Dakota truly trusted and treated me like an equal because I am feminine, because I act like a woman. You should rethink your look.

You think I was simply using him, but Agent Dakota and I truly loved each other *and* we had a profound understanding for one another. I was his number one asset and informant for the two Koreas and he was my lover and confidant. It's just insidious that I'm accused of espionage just because you caught me on the reversal route, Agent Park. But you know better than anyone else that I have to give North Korea some information to get some back for the US. That is the process, that is the price we pay. *(in Korean) I gave you all the maps that the agency has been using for the past 10 years. Where did you think all of that came from?**

And *now* suddenly I'm a traitor? A prospective murderer? Hardly. You know what I think? I think I became too threatening, being the one that knows the most and having had the heart of the most powerful man in the agency.

---

* (Pronunciation) Jee-nan ship-nyun dong-ahn dahng-shin-deul jo-jik-ee sa-yohng-hahn ji-do-nuen da neh-ga joon-guh-ra-go. Gu-geh-da uh-dee-suh na-wat-seul guh-ra-go saeng-gak-heh?
(Korean) 지난 10 년 동안 당신들 조직이 사용한 지도는 다 내가 갔다준 거라고. 그게 다 어디서 나타난 거라고 생각해?

So yes, I can give you the dates and times and which nuclear map I gave to Comrade Song. But no. I will not admit to being a traitor. Unfortunately, I only blame myself for not seeing this coming. It's happened before, why wouldn't it happen here? Because it's the land of the free…?

(beat) Those Mongolian desert nights, when I was on the run… were… bone chilling and heart crushing. Still, silent, desolate and very very starry. I should have expired there. I should of. Hope is a dangerous thing. False images in your mind can be very dangerous. I should know. I was creating those illusions as an actress for starving civilians to strive for the 'great cause'. We grew up on lies about South Korea. South Koreans were not starving and eating dirt. They had skyscrapers glittering in the sun, supermarket shelves stuffed with food. Those TV images that I had seen in China haunted me.

I guess that's why the North Koreans wanted to arrest me. For having seen. For knowing. For being cognizant. Agent Park, I'm continuously punished by the gods for 'knowing too much.' Is that a sin? You better be careful, too. You're not that unlike me.

Catherine starts humming the North Korean propaganda song "The Red Flag" from the previous scene. As she turns in the chair, she transforms into Agent Park.

SCENE 10: AGENT PARK / FBI INTERROGATION ROOM

AGENT PARK: *(finishing the last refrain)* Is that how that North Korean propaganda song goes? You sure do have a… poetic way of putting things. But let me just get the bare bone facts straight. You escape North Korea and work for South Korea against North Korea; then work for South Korea and the US as an informant; and then sell us both out to a country that screwed you over? And I'm supposed to believe that I caught you on the reversal, that you sold US defense information to actually help us? Yeah, right.

(Agent Park starts pacing) And really, you're lecturing me about love? You used your own daughter as a front for your spying, your lovers and husbands are expendable. You see, my mother sacrificed everything for me, her own career, her own life. And she would never put me in harm's way. So I'm the one that

understands what true love really looks like. Jesus, wake up.

Agent Park shakes her head as she transforms into Mina.

SCENE 11: MINA / SOLITARY CONFINEMENT

Mina paces like a caged animal in the solitary confinement room, whispering to herself.

MINA: Wake up. Wake up, wake up, wake up. *(shouts)* Wake up, Mom! It's like 1pm right now. I'm bored! I know you're jetlagged, but it's my summer vacation and you promised you'd spend some time with me.

She sits in the chair to talk with 'Catherine.'

So where did you go this time? Macau? Guatemala. Did you take any photos this time? Why don't you ever take any photos, Mom? Seriously, what happened to that digital camera I ordered for you on line? I mean I can upload that shit, stuff for you in a nano second on my computer. It's super easy. Geez,

Mom you can be so "2000 and late, I'm so 3008." It's a song from the Black Eyed Peas.*

Yeah, Dad came by last week when you were out of the country. We played Cranium and I totally won, so that was fun. But you know, he gets super moody and he totally misses you. So I had to listen to his depressing story again of when you guys first met, that he remembers exactly what you were wearing – a light pink dress with your black hair in a ponytail. Oh, but he used a new word this time that you looked quite *fetching*. Dad can be so mushy sometimes. Fetching?

(beat) I wish I were pretty like you. I know, I know, I'm special, I'm inter-racial, I'm a ying-yang product of the new millennia, I'm a mixed bag o' surprises from the placent-ee-a. But I'm not pretty, I don't look like you! No Mom, no one thinks I'm a pretty Asian girl, *(standing from chair)* everyone thinks I'm Hispanic! Cuz my eyes and hair's like this yucky brown color that just looks dirty… Your skin is so smooth and you have no body hair, and I have this dark fur mat all over me. And you don't have

---

* Alternate line: Geez, Mom, you can be so 90s, sometimes.

freckles. These are not cute, these dots that look like poo marks are not cute, Mom. How come I don't look like you and Dad? I mean Dad's not that good looking but at least his eyes are green. I'm just like this bad cake mixture that went wrong.

Mina sits back into chair.

What? "Divine organic creation?" Where'd you get that from? You're not just saying that, right? Yeah, that's totally way cooler and more important than just being pretty. And I guess my eyes are bigger and my lashes are longer than yours so...that part makes me a little bit prettier than you.

Mina cradles her face with both hands as if her mother is doing so. Then stands up and stares out.

Mom, hurry up and come save me...

She walks around to the back of the chair and starts putting on the cardigan, transforming into Mrs. Park.

SCENE 12: MRS. PARK / LIVING ROOM

MRS. PARK: My silly girl Ji-young. She was always fighting even when she was a young child. Tom boy, Tom boy. (she shadow boxes) Tough girl. But not because she is bully, but you know, it was hard for her growing up in the small town in Georgia. No Asians there.

I remember one afternoon, Ji-young came back home – hit all over her face, dress torn, nose bleeding. I shouted, "Ji-young-ah, what's wrong? What happened?" But Ji-young just stared at me. She did not even cry. Then she just said she had to take care of some 'bad boys'.

Then she went into the bathroom and grabbed the scissors. I was so scared she was going to hurt herself, so I ran after her and tried to take it away from her but she was already quite tall by then. She look at me and said "Umma, don't worry. I'm just going to cut my hair." I said, "Don't do that. You have such nice hair. Ji-young-ah, don't do that." But, she doesn't listen to me.

Then she just snip, snip, cut off her long beautiful hair. She stared at the mirror for a long time. I think she forgot I was there because she jumped when I came behind her to style her hair to look better. And I said, "You are right, Umma was wrong. Buddha says hair is the *weed of ignorance*. That's why monks are bald. You are too smart to be vain and carry around so much hair. I like this new hairstyle."

Of course, I was upset! My girl is so pretty and now she looks like that Peter Pan boy. But I wanted to acknowledge Ji-young's actions and kind of ritual, you know? Then I made a promise with her "Umma will not dye or pluck my grey hair so it reminds me of my old-age and impermanence, and keeps me humble too, okay?' And then we do pinky promise. Sealed with stamp.

Mrs. Park mimes a pinky promise, sealing it with her thumb.

But that's all I could do. Make a promise. I felt very very sad that I could not protect my daughter and give her all the things she deserved. But I was so tired working all the time. From prestigious professor to immigrant factory worker.

(*Sits in chair*) Anyway, so that's why I don't dye my hair. I know, I know I would look at least 15 years younger but I made that promise with Ji-young.

Mrs. Park leaves her sweater on the chair and turns into Agent Park.

SCENE 13: AGENT PARK / FBI INTERROGATION ROOM

Projection of a photo of Catherine holding Mina as a younger child. Agent Park grabs the same photo from her file.

AGENT PARK: This photo that you took in the States with your daughter Mina, what number face is this? Is this number five? Did you get your current face done here or in Seoul? They do have the best plastic surgeons in the world.

Agent Park, photo in hand, slowly pushes the chair forward and looks straight ahead into 'the mirror.'

Do you miss looking pretty? When you wake up in the morning and look yourself in the mirror, do you get confused with who you are? Doesn't it bother you that your daughter doesn't look like you?

As Agent Park's hand reaches out as if to touch Catherine's face, she sits immediately into the chair, transforming into Catherine. The photo still in hand.

SCENE 14: CATHERINE & AGENT PARK'S DUEL / FBI INTERROGATION ROOM

CATHERINE: *(as if swatting away Agent Park's hand)* Don't touch my face! You want to hear the rest of my amazing stories so you can put them in your FBI files and get promoted? Then don't ever touch my face.

Looks at the photo of her and daughter Mina.

Yes. This photo was taken in Los Angeles when she was five. Look, Agent Park, I'll tell you everything. I'll even give you my personal comprehensive analysis if you want. But you have to promise you'll protect me and my daughter.

Pause.

Okay. The South Korean National Intelligence
Service, that training was easy. I'd memorize a
Shakespeare play in a day, what, pretending to be
South Korean was going to take me time? I was fully
integrated in 5 months. I was trained in American
English, Chinese, Japanese, Russian and German. *(in
German)* Du hast dass auch getan, oder?*

I translated and decoded all information I had about
North Korea for the NIS, but most were from those
silly propaganda movies, so who knows what was
really true or not. But the South Korean NIS gobbled
up whatever information I gave them. I was the best
informant they had ever had. And so, I was treated
like royalty. Again.

"Oh, what a self-involved pathetic actress she is, she
needs attention." No Agent Park, it's much more than
that. I was deemed useless and harmful to my own
country. Just because the stupid son was threatened
by his father's former regime, he wiped out my entire

---

* You did too, right? (German alternate line) Du auch hast dass
an der akademie gelernt, oder? (English) You learned all that at
the Academy as well, right?

existence. So you can see how necessary it was for me to be South Korea's number one informant. To gain back a sense of – being.

Why do we feeble human beings struggle with this, this sense of existence? I mean at the end of the day, we just come and go, poof, it's all unreal, absurd. A cruel joke, really. And on top of that we have this thing called 'hubris'. That makes every thing so much worse. *(laughs)* You really do owe me. I'm giving you all these free lessons about love, life, being a real woman, and all the information you want about the Black Butterfly project. So now please, it's only fair for you to tell me where my daughter Mina is and what you've done with her.

As Catherine gets up from the chair, she transforms into Agent Park and takes the photo to the desk.

AGENT PARK: You really are an amazing actress, all these highfalutin words. But you still haven't told me anything concrete. You need to tell me which US nuclear map you gave to Comrade Song, how you stole it from Agent Dakota, and why you would do such a thing like that!

So don't get side tracked. Your daughter's fine. She's in solitary confinement, but she's being looked after. Of course, none of that is guaranteed.

Agent Park moves to left of chair.

See, you should of thought this through instead of being so selfish. So don't try and patronize me with your bullshit philosophy. Now if you were so invaluable for South Korea why did you decide to work for the US?

As Agent Park sits into the chair, she immediately transforms into Catherine.

Catherine speaks to Agent Park as if on her left. She talks while tracking Agent Park sitting down 'in front' of her.

CATHERINE: I did not make that choice! South Korea sold me off, as an asset to work for the FBI, so I could have even more access to North Korea, the US, the world. I never agreed to any of this. They both conspired to fake all my transcripts, IDs, records so I could pursue a graduate degree in the US. It's all true.

*(in Korean) What would you have done?** If you had such an allotment in life? Would you have killed yourself in Mongolia? Stayed in South Korea? Work for the US as an informant? Or supposedly betray everyone and sell out to a country that ruined your life?

Like I said, you're not that different from me. I think that's why you're so agitated and anxious – about me. I didn't have any agenda when this whole thing started. My fate was that I was born pretty, looking like Kim Jung-il's mother. That was my unfortunate allotment. After that, everything was a decision of the moment of choosing life instead of death, understand?

Catherine switches to Agent Park in chair.

AGENT PARK: Oh, fate, that favorite Asian excuse, fucking fate. Please. You *chose* to escape to North Korea, you chose to sell yourself as an asset, and you chose to throw away your life.

(stands up from chair) You know what I think? I think

---

* (Pronunciatoin) Dahng-shin-ee neh-ip-jahng-ee-rah-myun uh-duk-heh het-seul-ka? (Korean) 당신이 내 입장이라면 어떻게 했을까?

you're bitter. I think you're full of *hubris* – this word you and your daughter really enjoy using. And you wanted this crazy country that screwed you over to *need* you. So you were willing to sell out at the expense of everything – even your daughter, to satisfy your own, own... I don't know, ego's too weak of a word here. To satisfy your own, "existential smugness." *(peers into Catherine)* Am I right? *(slowly sits back down in chair)*

Agent Park switches back to Catherine.

CATHERINE: Label me all you want; spy, triple agent, confused actress with an identity crisis. But don't you dare accuse me of hurting my own daughter. Really, there was no master plan. And that is the unfortunate part of this all.

Suddenly, Catherine holds her heart in pain. Or is it Agent Park? While grunting, she transforms into Mina struggling to pull out an imaginary arrow stuck in her heart.

SCENE 15: MINA / SOLITARY CONFINEMENT

Mina finally pulls the arrow out.

MINA: So after I pull the arrow out that hit my heart, I also perform from another Greek tragedy called O-ee-dipus Rex. I don't know what the title means, but the quote is super cool.

Mina choreographs a dance while she recites.

"The tyrant – a tyrant's like a dickhead with a lot of power. The tyrant is a child of pride, who drinks from his great sickening cup recklessness and vanity, until from his high crest headlong he plummets to the dust of hope."

And who says Asian girls aren't expressive?

Piercing jail alarm. Mina cowers, covering her ears.

I hope... that's our pizza.

She goes to the door and looks through the peephole.

I told you – I don't know anything about my Mom's spying! And I wouldn't tell you even if I did. I'm hungry, bring me some food!

Dickheads!

Mina immediately transforms into Agent Park while walking over to the desk. She pulls a sheet out from her file.

SCENE 16: AGENT PARK / FBI Interrogation Room

AGENT PARK: You're charged for the following crimes.

Text projection of following statement on the back wall or screen.

United States Code Section 371; conspiracy to violate and defraud the United States for the purpose of impeding, impairing, obstructing, and defeating the lawful government functions of the IRS in the ascertainment, computation, assessment and collection of income taxes. And, United States Code Section 794; Unlawfully Delivering National Defense

Information to aid a foreign government.

Slowly walks towards the chair.

We naturalized you and hired you and trusted you to
work solely as a US informant. All your partying and
hobnobbing in those expensive hotels in Seoul was for
you to get verified information about North Korea's
nuclear reactors and what the hell is going on in
Youngbyun and their uranium, Mrs. White. That's
why we paid you over five million dollars with
money from people like my parents, hard earned
immigrant tax money, and we've just been
hemorrhaging that on you for the past 11 years!

Agent Park grabs the chair and turns it around to face her.

(*Hushed voice*) You know what they're saying? They're
saying "A pretty, petite, pansy looking gook like you
played us Americans like a yoyo. Who would of
thunk it?" And you have no idea what repercussions
that have on people like me. As high as my ranking
goes and as long as I work here in the system and
however much my Mom donates to her Community
Improvement Associations or whatever, we Asians,

thanks to crazy gooks like you, are always going to be looked at with suspicious eyes. Trust me, growing up in the South with a name like Ji-young that no one could pronounce in a Buddhist household, I know. Thank God it was me who pinned you down. Instead of another dumb white fuck who you could sleep with. Like your handler Agent Dakota. No *former* FBI Agent Dakota. Now you are a modern Mata Hari if I ever saw one. Somebody needs to make a movie out of you.

(beat) You know what they do to people like you now? A traitor and informant? To potential terrorists, post 911?

You're a highly educated, multi-lingual, philosophy spewing triple agent, so you must know the word "hamartia." No? Shame on you. Your daughter did a whole paper on it. It means "missing the mark." See, this hero, who could've had anything, has too much hubris. And that causes the hero's downfall into the inferno.

(in Korean) You might get your daughter killed. Think

about that.*

Agent Park walks over to the desk and puts the cardigan on, transforming into Mrs. Park.

SCENE 17: MRS. PARK / LIVING ROOM

Mrs. Park looks out at the audience and mimes a circle around her face.

MRS. PARK: You have nice face. Oh, you too. *(makes another circle around her face)* You know, Koreans read faces. *Gwan-sahng-hak.* Usually it's kind of silly. Like you. *(addressing an audience member)* "You have round back head and it's not flat, so you are smart." Or like you. *(points to another audience)* "You have long Buddha ears, so you will bring much luck to the company." Or like you. "You are very pretty, but look like cat, so she will eat up your husband." Something stupid like that. But at the same time, there is something about how one lives and how one looks.

---

* Ee-ruh-da-ga dahng-shin ddal juk-ee-get-uh. Jal-seng-kak-heh-bwa. (Korean) 이러다가 당신 딸 죽이겠어. 잘 생각해봐.

Look at my face. I don't have any wrinkles. *(pulls her hair back to expose her forehead)* No wrinkles on my forehead! That means, I didn't frown. I didn't frown for 66 years.* But today, I frown. Why? Because someone like John Yoo exist. And I read his face and he has fat neck and that is gluttony. *(in Korean)* Dukji dukji sal but-uh-suh mal-ee-ya. *(explaining)* You know, fat just slapped onto his neck. He actually looks like that North Korean fat boy leader. One must not trust people who look like that. I can't believe he is Korean, so embarrassing, jung-mal (really).

You don't know who John Yoo is? Oh boy, you must watch more PBS. He is the lawyer who wrote that controversial memo about the Patriot Act and advocated legal torture during Bush administration. He said, America does not have to abide by the Geneva Convention. I mean how can he say those things after seeing all those people being tortured in Abu Ghraib, uh? So, I did some research on the internet.

Mrs. Park walks over to the desk and looks through the file.

---

* Mrs. Park's age can change, depending on performance year's relation to the Korean War in 1950.

Uh-dee gaht-na…* Okay here it is.

Projection of text as Mrs Park reads from her note.

Geneva Convention. "Noncombatants, combatants who have laid down their arms, and combatants who are out of the fight due to wounds, detention, or any other cause shall in all circumstances be treated humanely, including prohibition of outrages upon personal dignity, in particular humiliating and degrading treatment. Women shall be especially protected against any attack on their honour, in particular against rape, enforced prostitution, or any form of indecent assault."

Internet! And people say, "But John Yoo, he must know, he graduated from Harvard, he graduated from Yale, he work in DC, he wrote a book, blah, blah." His parents are probably proud of him, but they should be ashamed. They are also war generation like me. How could they raise their child like that? I would disown a son like that. That's when you disown - not when your child marries a black

---

* Where is it... (Korean) 어디갔나…

person. Look at Hines Ward! He became Super Bowl MVP. Amazing.

So John Yoo is a professor at Berkeley? Ha! He is not a professor, *I'm* a real professor. He is, he is… a terrorist! Terrorist to the young mind and to humanity! And I wish my daughter could put him into jail!

(catching her breath) Ok, I have to calm down. I don't want to get heart attack or wrinkle because of stupid man like him.

Mrs. Park walks over to the desk. As she taker her cardigan off and leaves it on the desk, she transforms into Agent Park. Agent Park looks at a memo on her desk. Pause. Alarmed, she then hurriedly goes around the outside of the desk, and comes downstage center, to her superior's office.

SCENE 18: AGENT PARK / FBI OFFICE

AGENT PARK *(heatedly)*: Whaddya mean CIA is transferring her, transferring her where? She's my case. She is not an imminent threat, she doesn't have a frigg'n bomb strapped around her!

You don't understand sir. I've been working on this case, all by my self, barely sleeping for nine months. I busted my ass off to get us all the information about Comrade Song, dates of transactions, where she was when, when she did what, who she slept with, who she loved. I still need her to get to the bottom of Agent Dakota's death. One of our own was killed, sir. That's not CIA jurisdiction! What are they thinking? We need to find the perpetrator. One more day, I can get those reports... I'm not gonna just hand all my work over to CIA? They wouldn't even know what to do with all my stuff. They'd just use it against her.

I'm getting too close to her? She's my case. My subject. What, what are you taking about?

(beat) I chose to use Korean during the interrogation; it was a deliberate, calculated tactic. No, I was *not* siding with her, or empathizing with her, or "losing it." I did explain what was said during that interrogation, the translation is in the report, sir! Here, see…

Pause.

Who says... I can't be... trusted?

Agent Park tries to regain composure.

Sir. If we let the CIA take her out of this country, if she leaves this U.S. soil and goes to a foreign detainment camp, you know better than anyone else there's no way in hell she's coming back.

What about the little girl? Do you know where they're taking Catherine White? Sir, we can't let this happen…

Agent Park, dismayed and in disbelief, walks over to the chair and sits, her head buried in her two hands.

Shit…
Jesus Christ…

Agent Park slowly swivels the chair upstage, transforming into Catherine.

INTERLUDE / NETHERWORLD

Catherine is 'transported' out of the FBI interrogation room and into a prison cell that is part of a foreign detainment camp (or black site) in Thailand.

This can be expressed through conventions such as video projections, unidentifiable stagehand(s) acting as 'aggressor(s),' or a simple turn of the chair accompanied by a dramatic lighting change, as in the original production.

SCENE 19: CATHERINE / FOREIGN DETAINMENT CAMP IN THAILAND

Catherine's hands are bound back. She has been tortured. She slowly drags her feet as she turns the chair around while singing the South Korean song of resistance, "Morning Dew." As she slowly regains consciousness, she spots a foreign torturer.

CATHERINE: *(in Korean) Hey! Where am I?* *

---

* (Pronunciation) Yuh gi yo! Yuh giga uh-dee-jo?
(Korean) 여기요! 여기가 어디죠?

(in Japanese) Do you speak Japanese?*
Where is Agent Park!*

(in Mandarin) Do you speak Mandarin?*

How could she do this to me? She promised... Get me Agent Park! That coward... She promised. She promised she'd help me and my daughter! She's the only one who knows everything. You, you, you couldn't even being to understand...

I'm sorry. I'm sorry. You tell me what you've done to my daughter and I will tell you everything. I promise. You can do whatever you want to do with me.

Okay, okay. You want to play this game, then no more stories. Remember no one knows as much as I do.

---

* (Pronunciation) Ni hong go wah-ka-ri mas-uh-kka?
  (Japanese) 日本語が分かりますか？
* (Pronunciation) Agent Park wa do ko desuka?
  (Japanese) エージェント　パークはどこですか？
* (Pronunciation) Nǐ huì shuō zhōngwén ma?
  (Chinese) 你會說中文嗎？

Long pause. Catherine looks around and smells the stench in the cell.

"Here's the smell of the blood still. All the perfumes of Arabia can not sweeten this little hand."

Amazing character. I mean, everyone says that about Lady Macbeth. But I really didn't understand her until now.

"To bed, to bed: there's knocking at the gate. Come, Mina, come, come, come, give me your hand. What's done cannot be undone. To bed, to bed, to bed." *(in Korean) Mi-na ya, umma-ga jahl-moht-het-da. Umma-ga jahl-moht-het-suh…* *(in English)* I was wrong, Mina… Forgive me, I was wrong… .

Torturer comes closer to Catherine.

No, no, no… please… no…

---

* (Korean) 미나야, 엄마가 잘못했다. 엄마가 잘못했어…

SCENE 20: CATHERINE & MRS. PARK
/ NETHERWORLD

In slow motion, Catherine is kicked, beaten and tortured.

She spins in the chair.

Then she falls out of the chair onto her knees and lays sprawled on the floor.

Long pause.

Her hands start to slowly move into prayer position.

As Catherine slowly rises, she transforms into Mrs. Park giving Buddhist and Christian prayers on her knees.

MRS. PARK: *(in Korean, Buddhist mantra)* Nah-mu ah-mee tah-bool, gwan-se-eum-bo-sahl*

(in Korean, Christian prayer) Ju-yeh-soo-eul ee-reum-u-ro gi-do deu-ryut-na-ee-da.*

---

* (Korean) 나무아미타불 관세음보살.
* In the name of Lord Jesus, I pray. (Korean) 주 예수의 이름으로 기도드렸나이다.

Mrs. Park slowly rises. She gets her cardigan off the chair and puts it on her shoulders.

SCENE 21: MRS. PARK / LIVING ROOM

MRS. PARK: I never saw my daughter like this. She came home looking crazy, looking like she came from hell. I asked her "Ji-young-ah, what's wrong?" But she couldn't say anything. And I looked into her eyes and they were... empty. Then, I looked deeper. And inside I saw... sorrow. I remember seeing these kinds of eyes before.

That's why I don't like talking about the Korean War. Ji-young always asked me when she was younger. She took all those Asian American Pacific Islander heritage classes at University of Georgia. And knew what happened, on which date, and all historical details. But, of course, one can never really comprehend what it's like to experience a war.

(beat) When I was young, my family lived in Incheon. Yes, yes where the new international airport is right now. Nice airport, isn't it? Incheon is a very important

port city where General MacArthur, *(slowly enunciating) MacArthur* made his famous or infamous Incheon Sang-ryook Jak-jun, "Battle of Incheon," September 15, 1950. I was only four years old at the time. Incheon was also very famous because it had a big zoo and amusement park. So my first memory of the Korean war was very exciting. It was like Noah's arc and circus together right in front of my eyes. I remember being at the boardwalk with my mother and seeing all the animals being loaded onto this big big ship.

Tall giraffes, humongous elephants, monkeys, sheep, dog, wolves, cages and cages of animals.* I shouted to my mother, "Umma, Umma, look at that! Isn't it amazing? Isn't that exciting?" And I remember my mother looking down at me with these strange empty eyes. I had never seen my mother with this expression before, so her eyes looked empty. But actually they were very very sorrowful eyes. Very still. Very deep. And she hold my hand tightly.

It probably was some American ship since President

---

* Mrs. Park, ideally, should weave in and out of Korean as she lists the animal names.

Lee Seung-man was allied with the US, but who knows. I don't know where they were going. But they evacuated the animals first before the Korean people. The next thing I know, I was on the back of a jeep and going down to Busan. This is my first memory of the Korean War.

I never worry about my daughter. But this time, after seeing those eyes that reminded me of my mother's, I am worried. So, I went into Ji-young's room and read through her notes about the North Korean spy case.

I find it very interesting that the young daughter of the spy is pretending to shoot arrows. The investigation people and doctor have no idea what she is doing. But I think she is pretending to be *gimajok* – Korean Horse Warrior. The word Korea comes from Koryo, which was a powerful dynasty in the northern part of the peninsula connected to Mongolia. So gimajok were similar to Genghis Khan people – fierce Korean Horse Warriors. The girl must have heard some mythical stories about Korea from her mother.

I know the spy did something horrible. But it's very

wrong that they have the daughter under investigation by herself. The report also said that they are drugging her and that she seems a bit delusional.

Mrs. Park puts the shawl on the desk as she transforms into Mina.

SCENE 22: MINA'S WAR / SOLITARY CONFINEMENT & AGENT PARK / FBI OFFICE

Mina stomps over and sits in the chair.

MINA: Stupid dickheads! So I'm crazy cuz I keep speaking to my imaginary friend and my Mom? Like what am I suppose to do in this stupid room by myself anyway! *(erratically swiveling in her chair)* And like as if I'm going to give them any information about my mom. Hello? She my mom? She's not a spy! Just cuz she's Asian and speaks several languages does not mean she's a spy. That kinda logic is crazy.

Mina moves the chair towards the desk and immediately switches into Agent Park.

AGENT PARK: No I'm not crazy to resign, sir. What other choice to I have if the bureau is investigating all my reports, and my country is questioning my allegiance? That stands correct. I do not agree with how Catherine White and her daughter Mina are being treated.

As Agent Park pushes the chair away from the desk, she switches back to Mina.

MINA: They bust into our house, drag us both out of bed, my mom's trying to hold onto my hand, they put me in this stupid room and they try and give me pills and I'm...???

Mina hears a far away drum call, summoning her to battle. She slowly rises from the chair, turns the back of the chair to front and straddles it as if she is mounting a horse. She starts rolling around on 'the horse' and starts shooting arrows.

They just don't get it. I keep shooting at them, the real enemy, cuz I am taking them down! I am the fierce warrior, fighting against the savage tyrant. The blood thirsty dictator who drinks from his of sickening cup, recklessness and vanity and hubris and hamartia. Pyoong~!

The drum call gets louder and louders as Mina scans the horizon and sees her enemies coming towards her.

... Here they come!

Mina hides behind the chair and then hollers her warrior cry. She jumps out from behind the chair and prepares to shoot her last arrow with one last big inhalation.

SCENE 23: AGENT PARK / NETHERWORLD

Voice over of Thai operator connecting Agent Park's international phone call back home to Mrs. Park in the US.

Thai Operator: *(in Thai) "Thank you for using Tele Thai Prepaid International Calling Card. Please enter your 8 digit pin number, followed by the # key. We will connect your call shortly." * *

---

* (Pronunciation) Kor kob kun ti chai bor ri karn badt toh ra sub ra hwang prated Tele Thai cha nid tem ngern. Karuna kod mai lek PIN pead leag tarm duay kruang mai si liam. Ral ja tam karn cherm tor karn toh kong khun nai mai char.

Agent Park slowly crosses the stage towards the table. A gesture (gestus) in transitional light. She then puts on the cardigan and transforms into Mrs. Park.

SCENE 24: MRS. PARK / LIVING ROOM

MRS. PARK:

So the arrow flies.
Into the deep, dark void in time.

Where are you going my child?
Do the enemies still haunt you and hunt you down?

Into the horizon you ride.
With that traveling horse spirit you cannot hide.

Your arrowhead is bound to wound.
Scars will form, blood will congeal,
Hearts will be worn and spirits fatigued.

(Thai) ขอขอบคุณที่ใช้บริการบัตรโทรศัพท์ระหว่างประเทศ Tele Thai
ชนิดเติมเงิน กรุณากดหมายเลข PIN 8 หลัก
ตามด้วยเครื่องหมายสี่เหลี่ยม เราจะทำการเชื่อมต่อการโทรของคุณในไม่ช้า

You will succeed in targeting your bull.
But then what, my child,
Then what more can you do after such a kill?

MRS. PARK: I wrote this poem about the North
Korean spy case after Ji-young called me from
Thailand. My daughter is searching for some remote
detainment camp looking for the spy. She asked me to
find the young girl in some juvenile correction
hospital, but the connection was so bad I could not
understand everything.

Such strange times. Such odd news. I thought those
absurd times that can be so cruel and violent were
over when my family came to America. You know, I
love this country. It has protected me and my family
and given us so much. So it is just heart crushing, so
scary to think that some other immigrant family, who
is your neighbor, who lives right by you, you don't
know what they really do and suddenly they are
gone. And their existing life before is over.

Anyway, it's late now. Sorry to tell you such sad
stories, I really like you visiting, you are so quiet and
attentive and you have a good face, I like your face. I

hope my daughter Ji-young will come back home soon. So next time, you can meet her too.

Mrs. Park motions with her hand for people to leave.

Geu-reh, deu-ruh-ga-ra. Deu-ruh-ga.*

She starts leaving the stage and turns around one last time.

Go. Get home safely.

END OF PLAY

---

* Okay, go. Go home. (Korean) 그래, 들어가라. 들어가.

AFTERWORD

It was an early flight – 6:30 am to be exact. After Jet Blue flight 85 took off from JFK, I comfortably reclined my chair and fell fast asleep. I don't remember what exactly woke me up, except that I awakened with my shoulders in a startled hunched position and in a confused daze. I looked over to my left across the aisle, where an African-American man was staring at his small screen, watching live streaming TV, a novelty then. I hurriedly turned on my screen too. And there, I saw it.

On September 11th, 2001, as we flew from New York to Los Angeles, I watched the second World Trade Center tower fuming dark and disastrous smoke while the news anchor kept repeatedly emphasizing that what we were seeing was not a movie. Our flight was promptly ordered to land in Kansas City. I remember an older man (was he the same guy sitting next to me?) muttering, "Thank God the terrorists don't look like us." Hm. What if that terrorist did look like us, like . . . me, a harmless Asian woman? Like Hyun-hui Kim, the North Korean terrorist that took 115 lives on board the Korean Air flight 858 in 1985 when I was in elementary school? I would later realize that one of the characters in this play, Catherine, the alleged North Korean spy, evolved from that moment. And also from my life long fascination with espionage stories. I always wondered, "Would I have made a good spy?" and still have silly worries that the CIA will try to recruit me someday.

At that time when I left my New York City actor life, I had initially thought, "I'm just going to check out L.A. for a short while and see how it goes." But now with New York City so devastated and everyone still in shock, it seemed pointless to go back.

Several years into my L.A. life, in 2005, I received an exciting invitation. Roger Guenveur Smith, Peabody Award-winning actor and writer, called upon six writers/performers based in Los Angeles to develop 15-minute short solo performances using the facilities at the Mark Taper Forum (sadly, initiatives like these for artist of color no longer exist there). I've been a great admirer of Roger's work since I first ushered for his show A Huey P. Newton Story as a graduate student at the Yale School of Drama. I was grateful for this extraordinary opportunity where I got to develop my work with Roger and collaborate with talented colleagues.

In this workshop, <u>So the Arrow Flies</u> started out with three characters: Mina, the young hapa daughter; Catherine, her mother and alleged North Korean spy; and the FBI agent, Agent Ji-young Park. The short piece ended at a moment of suspenseful crescendo when Mina opens her front door to find FBI agents, who then invade her house and drag her mother away. I feel strongly about my characters – they are in depth, complex and contemporary Asian female roles rarely seen in Hollywood and theater at large. I thought, "I'll expand this 15-minute piece soon," but I didn't end up realizing that goal until a few years later.

***

It's the kind of phone call you never want to receive. That your mom, with whom you just spoke a few days before, was found unconscious on the floor. She went into a coma for five days, parts of her brain slowly dying. Henry Mayo Hospital's doctors had no clue what was going on with my mom. Our family was on high alert – our living room looking like a presidential campaign, with paper everywhere and everyone on different phones shouting, trying to find some way to help Mom. My dad called his best friend and leading infectious disease doctor in Korea, Dr. Seung-chul Park. After listening to her symptoms, he said that if she were his patient, he would not wait for lab results to come back but treat her with tuberculosis medication immediately. The Korean War had come back to haunt her in the most awful and harrowing way. Anyone who survived the Korean War has been exposed to tuberculosis. Most are inactive, but elders with compromised immune systems can develop the active form of the disease. In my Mom's case, it was an even rarer situation where it attacked the base of her brain, causing TB meningitis.

The sky was . . . strange.

Los Angeles skies rarely have clouds but that evening, at dusk as I was leaving the ER, all these small, spongy clouds had gathered overhead, like sheep in endless rows, reflecting shades of pink, light blue and orange. Had it rained? It was very pretty. I remember thinking, "Life undulates very, very oddly" and feeling a deep sense of melancholy.

During this high stress time of shuffling my mom from one hospital to another, two things happened. First, I created the fourth character, Mrs. Park, who serves as the narrator of the play as a dedication to my Mom and my parents' journey to the U.S. Second, instead of watching the comedy movie Knocked Up for some needed evening relief, as I had planned to do, I channel surfed and landed by chance on a searing documentary, The Ghosts of Abu Graib on PBS. The concoction of repressed stress and sadness related to my mom, listening to this documentary interviewees – especially the Arab prisoner talking bearing witness to his brother's torture – along with drinking lots of wine, I shed long and hard tears into the early morning.

These two occasions catapulted me into writing the bulk of the play in a flurry of three days at my kitchen table. A very interesting voice emerged for Mrs. Park and her daughter, FBI Agent Ji-young Park. They both started to reflect upon what it means to live in the U.S. as immigrants. And to struggle to survive, succeed and integrate as immigrants in their own perspectives. What is national identity in this globalized world and how do we navigate it? Mrs. Park became an angry citizen about the Bush Administration's prosecution of the so-called 'war on terror' and addressed the atrocities of war and of torture. And of kindness. I wanted to approach this hard topic in an intimate and artistic way where the audience empathizes with the fictional characters' experiences.

My mom, Inja Cho, pulled through – the result of what seemed nothing less than a series of miracles. She retained her old memories and recognizes my Dad, brother and I, but she has no short-term memory function. My friend, Michi, expressed it well when she said my Mom, in the truest Buddhist tradition, is always present in the moment. When I go visit her in the sub-acute unit of Encino hospital, she is *always* happy to see me.

***

When I was young, it wasn't the girly princesses in gowns stuck in castles that captured my imagination but rather the Hua Mulan-type princess warriors who took no prisoners on the battlefield. The title <u>So the Arrow Flies</u> emerged quickly as I recalled the old 5th century Korean fresco images of "Horse Warriors" (*gi-ma-jok*) I'd seen in history books as a child. I wanted to tie this Eastern idea of *gi-ma-jok* to the Western concept of *hamartia* in the play. The Greek word, *hamartia*, the fatal error of a tragic hero, literally translates into "missing the mark" in archery. Mina symbolizes these mythical ethoses of <u>So the Arrow Flies.</u> She expresses the concept of *hamartia* through her physical performances through out the play, and later embodies a Korean horse warrior – riding to battle armed with a bow and arrow, shooting down her enemies.

So the Arrow Flies. But to where?

The two heroines, Catherine and Agent Park, must struggle with this question. They must confront the choices they have made, as best they can, even at the expense of those choices becoming their hamartia. And perhaps, demise.

My journey with <u>So the Arrow Flies</u> has been unexpected, to say the least. I am proud that I have contributed to the effort to create more dynamic roles for women of color. And I am excited to continue to fly with the arrows to witness where it next aims, hits and lands with other artists and in different media forms.

Thank you for taking this special journey with me.

– Esther Chae
Santa Monica, CA

"Suryeopdo" (Hunting painting) from Muyong Tomb, Koguryo Dynasty (37 B.C. – 688 A.D.

<u>Acknowledgements & Special Thank Yous</u>

Acknowledgements to my fellow warriors
(in alphabetical order):

3 Hearts Productions Interns, Ars Nova Theater & production team, Arts Council of Korea (in particular Jin-kyung Kim and Junghoon Pi), Ricardo Acuna, Asian Women Giving Circle (in particular Melinda Chu, Hali Lee, Angie Wang), Michi Barall, Ed Bennett & BMS production team, Bridgette Buny, Brian Chae, Vic Chao, Cherry Lane Theater & production team (in particular Michael Sandoval, YaFang Cheng), Aiyoung Choi, David Chu, Ewan Chung, CUNY Martin Segal Theater (in particular Frank Hentschker, Kenn Watt), Maria Di Dia, East West Players (in particular Meg Imamoto), Chandler Evans, Scott Foster, Green Service Translation, Reme Grefalda, Melinda Hall, Joe Hernandez-Kolski, Velina Hasu Houston, Melinda Hsu, Chang-dong Lee, Corky Lee, David Jung, Jinny Jung, Larissa Kokernot, Piyanari Lefebvre, Mark Taper Solo Performance Workshop, Charles Mee, Erin Mee, Gwen Mihok, Miles Theater, Risa Morimoto, Oak Hill School (in particular Ki-Won Rhew), October Nights Festival & production team (in particular Silvia Grandi), Jeannie Park, Ping Chong

and Company, Jeanne Sakata, Luigi Santosuosso, Rosally Sapla, Sejong Society's production team (in particular Christian Oh), Jean So, Stage Left Studio (in particular Cheryl King) & production team, Tanne Foundation, TeAda Productions, TED Fellows Team, Paul Thompson, University of Michigan, Kyung Yoon, NetKAL (in particular Dr. Jehoon Lee and NetKAL 4), Wednesday Ladies Writer's Group, Wellesley College (in particular Esther Im).

A very special thank you (in alphabetical order):

Bruce Allardice, for being a true enabler; Master Ping Chong, for your artistic tutelage; Angela Cusack, for being my coach and cheerleader; Rena Heinrich, for being my intelligent comrade in the movement; David Henry Hwang, for paving the way and then pushing me through it; Boyoung Lee, for being my BFF and BA (Best Audience); Josslyn Luckett, for being my twin sister since the inception; Charles OyamO Gordon, my first and best playwriting teacher; Naomi Okuyama, for making it happen in the beginning; Anna Deavere Smith, for being my true artistic north; Roger Guenveur Smith, for the opportunity and inspiration; Casey Stangl, for being my trusted

director and sound board; Paul von Zielbauer, for
countless edits and endless encouragements.

For anyone whom I may have omitted, a hundred
bows. I remain grateful.

Notes on Contributors

David Henry Hwang's work includes the plays M. BUTTERFLY, CHINGLISH, GOLDEN CHILD, YELLOW FACE, THE DANCE AND THE RAILROAD, and FOB, as well as the Broadway musicals AIDA (co-author), FLOWER DRUM SONG (2002 revival) and DISNEY'S TARZAN. He is also America's most-produced living opera librettist. Hwang is a Tony Award winner and three-time nominee, a three-time OBIE Award winner and a two-time Finalist for the Pulitzer Prize in Drama. He won the 2011 PEN/Laura Pels Award, the 2012 Inge Award, the 2012 Steinberg "Mimi" Award, and a 2014 Doris Duke Artist Award. Hwang was recently the Residency One Playwright at New York's Signature Theatre, which produced a season of his plays, including the premiere of his newest work, KUNG FU.

Esther K. Chae is an award-winning actor, writer and TED fellow based in Los Angeles and New York. Her artistic work has been seen and heard on stage, television and film in the United States, Korea, Ireland, Australia, Canada, Italy, Nigeria and Russia. Her other plays include AE-RI IN OTHERLAND, featuring Korean percussion music 'samul-nori' and DDAN DDA DDAN!!!, an absurd short play about a superwoman socket puppet and her struggles. Chae graduated from the Yale School of Drama (MFA in Acting), the University of Michigan (MA in Theater Studies), and Korea University. She served as the Martin Luther King, Jr./Cesar Chavez/Rosa Parks Visiting Professor (University of Michigan), keynote speaker for the Arts Council of Korea and as a visiting artist at the Institute on the Arts and Civic Dialogue, founded by Anna Deavere Smith, at Harvard University. Chae was born in Eugene, Oregon, grew up in Seoul, Korea, and has traveled all over the world. She has climbed Machu Picchu, the Indian Himalayas and Mt. Kilimanjaro. She lives with her husband Paul von Zielbauer in Santa Monica, CA. www.estherchae.com

Korean Translations by Dae-hwan Kim and Soo Hye Jang.

Back cover headshot by Takemi photography.

그리하여 화살은 날아가고
SO THE ARROW FLIES

모노드라마
연출, 극본, 출연

에스터 채 (채경주)

공연 시간: 약 85 분

등장 인물:

캐서린 박- 북한 스파이 혐의자, 30 대
박지영 - 한국계 미국인 FBI 요원, 20 대
미나 화이트 - 캐서린의 혼혈아 딸, 12 살
박 여사 - 박지영 요원의 이민자 어머니, 60 대

시간배경: 현재

장소배경: 박 여사의 거실, FBI 취조실, FBI 사무실,
독방, 해외 수용소, 구천 혹은 연옥 세계

무대 위에는 작은 책상과 회전식 사무용 의자가 있다. 책상 위에는 녹음기, FBI 파일 하나, 펜 한 개, 물 한 잔이 놓여있다.

장면 1: 박 여사 / 거실

박 여사: *(무대 밖에서)* 그래, 지영아. 알았다~.

박 여사**입장한다. 활발한 성격의 60 대 한국 이민자.*

박 여사: 안녕하세요! 오, 그래 왔어? 아이고, 기다리게 해서 미안합니다. 우리 딸 지영이를 소개시킬려고 했는데, 글쎄 이 녀석이 방금 전화를 걸어 퇴근이 늦어져 저녁 식사는 같이 못 할 것 같다고 그러네요. 요즘 아주 열심이거든요, 엄청 중요한 북한 스파이 건을 맡고 있답니다. 내가 말씀 안 드렸나? 내 딸 지영이는 FBI 요원이랍니다. F, B, I. 미, 연방, 수사국! 캬! 이름부터 쿨하지 않아요?

내 이대 동창들은 지영이를 좀 무서워해요. 하루는 지영이가 바쁜지 겉옷도 안 걸치고 계단을 뛰어내려오는 바람에 옆구리에 총을 차고 있는 모습을 봤거든요. 그래서 친구들이 "어머나! 지영이 총 갖고 다녀?" 물어보길래 내가 그랬죠. "아니 FBI 요원 아냐~ 총 갖고 다니지, 그럼 뭘 갖고 다녀, 바나나?"

(의자에 앉는다) 대체 뭘 그리 무서워하는지 모르겠어요. 총 갖고 다녀서 그런가? 미국 코쟁이들이랑 같이 일해서? 아직 결혼 안 해서? 혹시 게이일까봐? 아니면 그 바보같은 밤송이머리 때문에?

---

*역자 주: 원작 연극에서 박 여사 캐릭터는 한국어 억양이 섞인 영어를 사용하나, 대학 교수 출신으로 그 구조와 내용은 결코 어눌하지 않습니다. 활발한 성격과 한국 교수 출신으로 공장에서 일한 이주 노동자라는 특징을 감안해 내용은 있으되 가벼운 듯한 말투를 사용했습니다. 이하 역자 주.

내 생각엔 바로 그 밤송이 머리 스타일 때문이라구요.
내가 항상 얘기하죠. "지영아! 티비 드라마 CSI 에
나오는 여자들 좀 봐라. 머리 얼마나 이쁘게하고
나오니?" 하튼 내 말 들질 않아요. 하지만 난 또
이해한답니다. 여러분도 아시겠지만 지영이가 보통
예쁜 게 아니잖아요. 그런 미인과 일하면 남자들이
집중을 못해요. 그러니까 좀 덜 꾸미고 튀지 않아야
하는 거죠. 무슨 말인지 알죠?

하지만 지영이가 눈에 띄지 않아야 하는 진짜 이유는
따로 있답니다. 그 애가 하는 일이 나쁜 놈들을 감옥에
쳐 넣는 일이잖아요. 그런데 가끔씩 그 사람들이
감옥에서 나와 요원들한테 복수하러 찾아오는 경우가
있답니다. 지영이는 악당들이 찾아올 경우를 대비해,
범죄자들 얼굴사진을 카피해서 책상에 놓아 두고는
자주자주 챙겨본답니다. (목소리를 낮춰서) 그래서
나도 몰래 지영이 방에 들어가서 그 카피를 또
카피했죠. 나도 한 사람, 한 사람 얼굴을 익히는 거죠.
눈은 무슨 색인지, 콧대는 얼마나 높은지, 턱 선은
어떻게 생겼는지...

내가 눈치가 빠르거든요. 눈치. 아하, 영어에는 이
말이 없어서 참 불편하다니까. 그러니까... "아이~
센스". (눈을 가리킨다) 주변을 살펴보고 일이 어떻게
돌아가는지를 잘 아는 눈의 감각. 난 이렇게 눈치가
빨라서, 만약 내가 사진에서 본 악당들을 보면, 딸
애한테 전화를 하거나, 경찰에 보고를 하거나, 그
나쁜놈들 주의를 흐트리거나, 뭐 어떤 수를 써야겠죠.
말하자면 내딸을 엄호하는 또 다른 비밀요원! 하,
여러분이 지금은 웃을지 모르겠지만, 아직 너무
어려서 이해못하는겁니다. 이런 게 다 엄마
마음이니까. 이게 바로 딸을 내가 위해 할수있는
일이니까요.

박 여사, 가디건를 벗어 의자에 놓는다. 의자를 무대

윗쪽으로 돌리고 일어나 박 요원으로 분한다.

장면 2: FBI 요원 박지영 / FBI 취조실

박지영 FBI 요원. *20 대 후반의 한국계 미국 여성.*
녹음기를 켜자 여자가 북한 사투리로 남자에게 말하는
소리가 들린다.

녹음기 소리.

송동무: 박동무 수고 많았습네다.
박동무: 아닙네다
송동무: 동무가 준 비밀정보는 바로 상부기관에
　　　　보고했습네다.
박동무: 알았습네다.
송동무: 곧 검은나비에게 연락드리겠습니다.
박동무: 네.

녹음기를 끈다.

박 요원: 녹음된 내용 대부분은 북한 남성의
목소리지만, 지금 들린 다른 사람 목소리는 당신
같은데, Mrs. 화이트?

의자(캐서린)를 향해 말한다.

우리 워싱턴 정보국에서 당신이 작년 6 월 12 일
서울에 있을 때 한 이 대화를 녹취했어. 김 대통령

---

* 대본과 실제 원작 연극 모두에서 박지영 요원은 미국 남부 억양 (약간 구식이고
남성스러우며 딱딱하게 들리는 말투)를 사용합니다. 번역본에서는 한국어를
사용하므로 성격을 고려해 가급적 딱딱한 남성적 말투를 사용했습니다.

연회장 위치를 알아내기 위해서 건 전화내용도
들었고, 당신을 친구라고 믿는 높으신 나으리들한테
꽃 배달을 시키려고 꽃집에 전화한 것도, 전부 다
들었지. 아, 물론, 우리는 당신 같은 우리 쪽 정보원들
전화를 보통 추적하거나 도청하지는 않지. 그래서
이걸 듣고 깜짝 놀라고 어리둥절 했단 말이야. 아니,
도대체 왜 우리 정보통이 북한 남자와 대화를 하고
있는걸까.

이런 짓을 할 이유가 뭐지? 그리고, 당신을 다정하게 "
박 동지"라고 부르는 이 남자, "송 동지"는 대체
누구지?

(비트) 여기에 대한 수사 협조는 영어로 해
주셔야겠는데요, Mrs. 화이트.

(파일을 집어 든다) 자... 당신의 다양한 이름들을
보자고, Mrs. 화이트. 본명 박승희, 1967년 북한 나진
출생. 중국에서도 박승희로 활동하다가 남한에 가서는
박혜경으로 이름 바꿈. 미국에 온 이후에 이민국에
등록하고 결혼 전까지 사용한 이름은 또 다른 캐서린
박. 미국에서는 성이 뒤에 오니까. 그리고 이 녹음
테이프에서는 당신을 "박 동지"라 부르고 또 암호명은
블랙 버터플라이, 검은 나비라고 부르는군. 그리고
이혼 후에는 남편성을 계속 쓰면서 캐서린 화이트라는
이름을 썼고. 세상에, 당신 도대체 이름이 몇 개야?
다섯? *(파일에서 이름을 세어본다)* 어, 미안. 여섯 개.
(비트) 이런, 나랑 똑같은 박씨라니...

*박 요원, 캐서린의 얼굴을 유심히 살핀다. 그리고는
그녀의 FBI 파일에서 지금의 얼굴과는 다른 캐서린의
흑백 사진을 꺼내어 캐서린에게 보여준다. 사진에서*

*캐서린은 북한 제복과 모자를 쓰고 있는 모습이다.
무대 뒷벽에 박 요원이 들고 있는 사진과 동일한
사진이 비춰진다.*

이름 수 만큼이나 다른 얼굴들을 가지고 있나, Mrs.
화이트? 당신이 북한 인민극장에서 "일호배우"로
활동하던 시절에 찍은 사진을 찾아냈어. 그래, 난
당신이 평양에서 배우 생활을 했다는 걸 알아냈단
말이야.

*FBI 취조실 창문을 향해 사진을 무대 오른쪽으로
보여준다.*

이봐, 어떻게 이렇게 중요한 걸 놓칠 수가 있는 거지?

자, 그럼. 이제 당신 성형수술 얘기부터 시작해 볼까?

*박 요원, 천천히 의자에 앉는다. 의자를 관객 쪽을
향해 돌리면서 캐서린으로 분한다.*

장면 3: 북한 스파이 캐서린 / FBI 취조실

캐서린, 30 대 후반의 북한 스파이 혐의자. 수갑을 찬
채로 다리를 꼬고 사진을 들고 앉아있다. 미국 표준
영어와 남북한 한국말 방언을 모두 구사한다.

---

*캐서린은 북한 출신이나 남북한 말씨를 고루 사용하고 표준 영어를 구사합니다.
원작 연극의 한국어 대사에서는 남한 말씨를 사용하므로 특별한 경우를 제외하고
기본적인 어투는 남한으로 정했습니다. 다만, 고향이 북한이므로 남북한을
지칭할 때는 (북)조선, 남한으로 표기했습니다.

캐서린: 애 많이 썼네... 아니 이건 또 어디서 찾았어,
그래. 저기 우리 물 좀 마시고 얘기하자구요. 뭐?
좋아. 영어로 답변해야만 물 준다면 영어로
얘기해주지. 비록 당신이 북조선말이나 남한 말을 둘
다 알아듣는 다는걸 알고있지만. (박 요원을 위아래로
훑는다.) 젊은 한국계 미국인 여성이 FBI 요원이라...
재미있네. 같은 박씨라, 우리 혹시 친척일지도
몰르겠네.

캐서린, 손에 든 흑백사진을 본다.

정말, 내가 봐도 김정숙이랑 똑같이 닮았었는걸.
성형수술을 언제 했냐고? 몇 번째 수술 말이야? 내
얼굴은 당신 이빨 개수보다 더 자주 바뀌었다고.

사람들은 내가 김정일 장군님의 어머니인 김정숙
동지를 빼다 박았다고 했지. 하지만 말이야, 진짜로
선전 영화에서 조선인민의 어머니 역을 맡기 위해서는
그냥 닮은 것만으로는 안 되지. 진짜 김정숙이 되어야
했지. 나는 조선민주주의인민공화국의 영광스런
"일호배우"로 부름 받았으니까.

캐서린, 사진을 무릎에 내려놓고 그녀의 얼굴에서
수술한 부분들을 가리키며.

독일 뮌헨의 Dr. 질바우어는 내 눈매, 이마 폭, 귀
크기가 김정일 장군님의 어머니랑 일치한다고 했지만,
완벽하게 똑같으려면 여기저기 손을 좀 봐야 했지.
콧구멍을 더 가름하게 1.5 밀리 올리고, 광대뼈도 좀
채워 넣고, 턱 선은 날카롭게, 가슴은 더 작게. 아,
그리고 제일 중요한 부분. 내 목소리.

캐서린, 손짓을 한 채 북한의 선전가요 "적기가"를 부른다.

"높이 들어라 붉은 깃발을, 그 밑에서 굳게 맹세해!"

정말이지 끝내주는 일이었어. "태양은 영원히 빛난다"에서 경애하는 지도자의 어머니, 김정숙 동지의 젊은 시절을 연기할 때 내 나이, 겨우 열일곱. 후끈 달아오른 열정적인 공연, 환상적인 매스게임, 온 경기장에 도배된 내 얼굴, 유럽이랑 러시아에서 수입해 온 값비싼 음식과 와인. 모두가 우리 일호배우들을 사랑했어. 그래야만 했지. 그게 그들의 의무였으니까.

캐서린, 무릎에서 사진을 집어 든다.

오늘은 모국의 어머니, 내일은 헌신했던 국가에 쫓겨 다니는 망명자. 하! 인생은 정말 웃기게 꼬인단 말이야. 안 그래, 박 요원?

캐서린, 사진을 바닥에 던진다.

자, 그럼 이제 내 딸 미나를 어떻게 했는지 말해.

장면 4: 박 요원 / FBI 취조실

박 요원, 바닥에서 캐서린의 흑백사진을 집어 든다. 그리고는 책상으로 걸어가 FBI 파일을 연다.

박 요원: 당신 딸은 안전해. 형식상 그냥 이것저것
물어보고 있을 뿐이야. 그보다 먼저 우리 얘기를
계속해 볼까?

*박 요원이 파일를 검토하면서 김일성 일가의 가계도가
무대 뒷 벽에 비춰진다.*

1994 년, 제 1 대 독재자 김일성 사망. 그 아들
김정일로 체제 이양. 그 후 조선인민의 어머니 축출.
아니지, 바로 당신, 조선인민의 어머니 김정숙역을
연기하던 배우 축출. 제 2 대 독재자, 김정일이 전
아버지의 가계를 깨끗이 정리하고 자기만의 체제를
세우기 위한 수안이였지. 자, 이제 김정일도 죽었고,
이제는 그 아들 김정은이 북한 최고사령관이 되었다.
기가 막히는 구만...

1994 년, 바로 그 해에 당신은 중국과 북한 사이 국경
감시원으로 추방됐는데, 거기서 도망쳤지. 우선 중국
본토로 들어가서 얼굴을 다시 한 번 뜯어고쳤어.
그래야 사람들이 김정숙을 연기한 당신 얼굴을
알아보지 못할 테니까.

*박 요원, 처음 꺼냈던 흑백사진과 또 다른 컬러 사진을
함께 꺼낸다. 그 사진 또한 캐서린의 예전 얼굴 중의
하나이다.*

안됐네. 꽤나 예쁜 얼굴이었는데. 그 중국 의사,
얼굴을 못생기게 만드는 기술 하나는 좋은데.

책상으로 돌아가 두 사진을 모두 FBI 파일에 넣는다

당신은 다시 몽골로 도망쳤고, 그곳에서 한국
대사관에 들어가는데 성공해서 서울로 가게됐지. 한국
신문에서는 이렇게 보도했더군. "조선인민의
어머니조차 고통스럽고 피폐한 삶을 견디지 못하다."
한국의 국정원은 아주 신나서 당신을 정보원으로
고용했고. 맞나?

*박 요원, 책상에 놓여져 있던 물잔을 들어 길게 한
모금을 마신다.*

이틀 전 다코타 요원이 숨진 채 발견되었어. 바로
김정일 사망 직후에. 좀 이상하단 말이야. 왜 그런지
혹시 알고있나?

박 요원, 즉시 미나로 분한다.

장면 5: 미나 / 독방

*미나,*캐서린의 12세 딸로 한국인과 백인의
혼혈이다. 미나, 의자 뒤에서 함성을 지르며
뛰어다니고, 마치 전투를 재현하듯 무대 여러곳을
향해 보이지 않는 화살을 겨눈다. 화살을 쏘며.*

미나: 퓽~ 퓽~ 퓽!

*미나, 갑자기 가상의 화살들을 맞는다. 마지막 화살은
그녀의 심장에 꽂힌다. 휘청거리다가 의자에 털썩
주저앉아 죽어가며.*

----

* 미나는 총명하고 발랄한 성격이나 결코 착하기만 한 어린아이는 아닙니다.
극중 인물 중에서 가장 욕설이 많은 캐릭터이기도 합니다. 굳이 일부러 표현을
순화하기보다는 가급적 적절한 단어를 찾아서 사용했습니다.

미나: "하... 하, 하마티아..."

미나, 의자에 축 늘어진다. 비트. 다시 일어나 묶은 머리를 매만지고는 '가상의 절친한 친구'와 대화하듯 관객을 향해 이야기를 시작한다.

미나: 바로 이렇게 했다니까! 그리스 비극 숙제 말이야. 아, 물론 쿠퍼 선생님도 완전히 뻑가서 A+ 를 주셨지. 이 그리스 비극 숙제를 레포트가 아닌 연극으로 표현해서 발표 할 생각은 아무도 못했거든. 자, 봐. 그러니까 내가 온몸에 화살을 맞고 죽은 다음에, 아리스토텔레스의 시학(詩學)에 나오는 하마티아에 대해서 설명하는 거야.

하, 마, 티, 아. 이게 무슨 뜻인지 알아? 원래는 활쏘기에서 "과녁을 놓치다"라는 뜻인데, 그리스 비극에서는 영웅의 치명적인 실수, 결함, 그런 뜻으로 쓰인대. 과녁을 하나 놓친 게 치명적인 실수가 되는 거지. 보통 그런 건 자만심 때문이야. 자만심은 뭔지 알지? 음... 그러니까 자만심은 자신감이 너무 많은 거야. 니가 뭐든지 할 수 있다고 생각하고, 다 니 맘대로 해도 된다고 생각하는 것 처럼 말이야. 그리고 자만심이 너무 넘치면, 또라이가 되는 거라구. 마이클 림버처럼.* 그 자식은 지 아빠가 국회의원인가 뭔가가 된다면서 아주 잘난 척 하지만, 우리 반 애들은 전부 그 자식을 완전 싫어하잖아. 또라이니까. 또~라~이. *(춤을 춘다)* 선생님들도 걜 싫어한다니까. 진짜야.

미나, 책상 쪽으로 걸어오며 박 요원으로 분한다. 박 요원, 책상에 놓여진 메모를 읽은 후 파일을 집어

---

* Rush Limbaugh 의 성을 따옴. 또는 다른 현 미공화당의 맹목적 우익정치인의 성을 붙여도 된다.

들고, 책상 밖으로 돌아 무대 앞쪽 중앙으로 걸어와 상사의 사무실에 들어선다.

장면 6: 박 요원 / FBI 사무실

박 요원: 네, 과장님. 저희가 캐서린한테 검은 나비 암호명 아래 북한에게 제한된 정보를 주라고 한 것은 맞습니다. 하지만 그 기밀 문서를 전부 넘겨주기로 한 것은 아닙니다. 아니, 핵 프로그램에 종사하는 연구진 이름과 얼굴이 담긴 서류를 줬다는게 말이 안돼죠. 그리고 캐서린이 유출한 사진 중에 다코타 요원의 환갑 파티때 사진도 들어있습니다. 과장님을 비롯해서 FBI 핵심 요원들의 얼굴들이 다 찍힌 사진 말입니다. 기억하실지 모르겠습니다만, 그 사진을 찍은 건 캐서린의 딸 미나였습니다. 순진한 꼬마아이가 가족사진을 찍는 것처럼 보이게 한거죠.

제 생각에는 캐서린과 다코타 요원이 연인 사이가 된 것이 북한 측에서 다코타 요원을 살해한 주 원인인 것 같습니다. 하지만 그런 명령이 새 정권 하에서 내려진 것인지는 잘 모르겠습니다. 그렇게까지 빨리 움직이지는 못했을 것 같은데 말입니다.

과장님, 캐서린의 딸은 집으로 돌려보냈습니까? 네? 하지만 미성년자를 그런 식으로 심문하는 것은 위법일텐데요. 자칫하면 큰 문제가 될지도 모릅니다. 시간이 없는 건 알고 있습니다만, 지금 녹음 테이프를 듣고 정보를 찾아내는 작업은 저 혼자 하고 있잖습니까. 서울, 평양, 워싱턴에서 녹음된 것만 해도 200 시간 분량이 넘습니다.

CIA 요? 아니, 그 작자들이 원하는 게 뭐죠?

박 요원, 책상으로 돌아가 파일을 던진다. 의자에 걸린
가디건를 집어 들고 어깨에 걸치고는 박 여사로
분한다.

장면 7: 박 여사 / 거실

박 여사: 난 우리 딸 지영이가 너무 너무 자랑스럽죠.
그 애는 FBI 최연소 여자 요원 중 하나랍니다.
엄청나죠? 우리 아이가 미국 정부를 위해서 일한다는
게. 우리 같은 이민자들이 미국 사회의 진정한 일원이
되는 건 바로 '영어'로 이 나라를 대표할 수 있게 되는
순간이에요. 내가 알죠. 난 한국에 있을 때 언어학
교수였으니까.

과학자나, 기술자나, 의사말고. 말하자면, 변호사 같은
직업 말입니다. 재판에서 이기려면 쉴새 없이
이야기하고 멋들어진 주장을 펴야 하잖아요. 아니면
배우. 아니 아니, 대사 한 마디 없는 엑스트라 말고
가슴을 울리는 멋진 캐릭터를 소화해 내는 그런 배우.
음, 이름이 뭐더라... 아, 조안 첸. "마지막 황제"에서
정말 멋있었잖아요. 어쩜 그렇게 내 마음을 잘 아는지.
그 여자는 우리나라 사람이 아닌 중국 사람이지만,
괜찮아요.

그게 아니면 FBI 요원. 수많은 사람들과 대화를
하면서 '내가 미국을 대표하고 있다'는 확신을 줘야 그
사람들이 중요한 정보를 줄 것 아니겠어요. 그러니까
외국 엑센트가 있는 영어를 쓰고 미국인처럼 행동하지
않는 사람들은 FBI 요원이 될 수 없다고 생각해요.
우리는 예전에 조지아 주에 살아서 지영이가 좀
독특한 남부엑센트가 있기는 하지만 그건

미국사람처럼 들리니까 문제가 없죠. 무슨 말인지 아시죠?

(의자에 앉는다) 아, 재미있는 얘기 하나 해 드릴까? 지영이가 버지니아주에 있는 FBI 훈련소에서 교육 받을 때, 사격 교관이 한국 사람이었대요. 그 남자 영어가 좀 서투른데, 흥분하면 더 심해졌다네요. 어느 날 훈련생들이 사격 연습을 하고 있었는데, 저 멀리있던 마네킹이 급하게 다가오니까 지영이가 겁먹고 완전 얼어붙어서 총을 못 쏘고 있었더래요. 그래서 그 한국인 교관이 "지영, 뭐 하는 거야! 쓰로요 건 (throw your gun), 총을 던져!"라고 외쳤대요. 그러니까 지영이가 완전 헷갈려서 권총을 빼서는 마네킹에 던져 버렸대요, 글쎄. 사실 그 교관은 "총을 뽑아! 드러우 유어 건 (draw your gun)!"이라고 말했어야 하는건데. 드,러,우. 에그, 그걸 헷갈려 듣다니, 멍청한 녀석. 세상에 누가 과녁에 총을 집어 던진단 말이에요?

나도 내 영어에 한국 엑센트가 있다는 걸 알아요. 하지만 난 영어가 꽤 유창한 편이랍니다. 영어로 시도 쓰구요. 아마 대부분의 미국인보다 영어를 더 잘 쓸걸요? 하지만 걔네들은 그걸 잘 몰라요. 나만 보면 "아휴, 동글동글 귀여워, 아이고 웃겨, 웃긴 엑센트 있네" 라고 하지요. 제가 무슨 말을 하든 선소리로 생각한다니까요. 쓸데없는 잡담. 선소리. 스틸틸로퀴(stutiloquy). 여러분, 이 라틴어 뜻 모르셨죠?

(손목시계를 본다) 아, 얘기가 길어졌네요. 지영이는 못 온다고 했으니 기다리지 말고 저녁이나 먹읍시다.

박 여사, 앉은 채 무대 뒷쪽으로 의자를 밀면서 동시에 가디건을 의자등에 벗으며 미나로 분한다.

장면 8: 미나 / 독방

미나: 으, 배고파. 사람을 데려다 놨으면 밥을 줘야 할 거 아니야? 피자...면 좋겠는데

미나, 초조해하며 무대 앞 왼쪽의 '유치장 문'을 엿본다. 유치장 안을 돌아다니며 '가상의 친구'에게 다시 말을 건다.

어, 엄마는 집에 계신데... *(짐짓)* 몸이 별로 안 좋아서 누워 계셔. 우리 엄만 너희 엄마처럼 요리 잘 안 하는 거 알잖아. 그래, 요리를 못 하는 동양 엄마는 울 엄마 뿐일거야. 휴, 이게 뭐람.

의자등을 앞으로 돌려 앉는다.

근데 웃긴 게 뭔지 알아? 울 엄마 성격이 되게 쎄거든. 그래서 아빠랑 이혼할 때도 하나도 안꿀렸어. 또 엄마를 무시하는 사람들은 끝까지 말로 싸워서 이겨버리지. 그래 놓고 나한테는 항상 "니가 엄마를 돌봐야해" 그러신다. 웃기지? 나는 엄마를 지키는 전사라나? 왜냐하면 난 아무도 엄마를 건드리지 못하게 보호해드리거든. 왜냐면... 난 모든 걸 알아. 우리 엄마가 세계 평화를 위해서 아주~아주 중요한 일을 하는 고위급 대사라는걸. 그거, 아주 위험한 일인 거 알지? 게다가 사람들은 여자, 특히 유색인종에다가 똑똑하고 예쁘기까지 한 여자를 싫어한다구. 위기감을 느끼는 거지. 오프라 윈프리가 티비에서 그랬어. 그게

바로 우리 엄마라니까. 너랑 나랑도 나중에 크면
그렇게 되는거야.

의자에서 일어난다.
야, 당연히 나도 포함되는 얘기지. 혼혈아라고 내
얘기는 아닌 줄 알아? 언제나 특징 있고 개성 있는
유색인종이 맹물같은 백인피보다 쎄다는거 몰라?

알아... 내 이름 미나 화이트라는거. *(앉는다)* 나랑
진짜 안 어울리는 바보 같은 성이야. 18 살이 되면
무조건 이름을 미나 박으로 바꿀 거야. 넌 아마 모를
텐데, 미나라는 이름은 영어 이름으로만 들리지만
사실 한국말로도 아주아주 깊은 뜻을 갖고 있다구.
엄마가 그러는데 미,나 -

*허공에 대고 '미나'라고 한글로 쓴다. 동시에
한글/중문 글자가 애니메이션으로 벽에 비춰진다.**

- 라고 하면 중국 글자로 "예쁘고 아름답다"는
뜻이래. 멋지지 않니? 흠, 한국 이름이 왜 중국어로
뜻을 다는지는 잘 모르겠는데... 우린 중국사람이
아닌데. 엄마가 일어나면 물어봐야겠다. 하지만
지금은 엄마가 긴~ 여행 끝에 집에 돌아온 참이니까,
그냥 주무시게 나둬야해.

*미나, 휴식을 취하는 것처럼 눈을 감고 캐서린으로
분한다.*

---

* 美娜

장면 9: 캐서린 / FBI 취조실

캐서린: 당신 한 번이라도 배고파 본적 있나?
그러니까, 진짜로 굶어 죽을 것 같은 느낌 말이야.
고위급 관리직에서 배급이나 타 먹는 국경 감시원
꼴이 되다니. 난 정말로 보통 인민들이 이렇게 사는지
몰랐어. 사상 최악의 기근이 북한을 덮친 뒤로는 훨씬
심각해졌지.

내가 아직까지 살아있는 건 그 사람 덕분이야.
일호배우 시절에 당에서 짝지어준 북한 남편.
고맙게도 아주 좋은 사람이었어. 얼음장처럼 차가운
두만강을 헤엄쳐 넘어와서는 도망치라고 말해줬지.
내가 남한 사람들이랑 어울린 죄로 기소되었다면서.
하지만 국경으로 날 추방한 건 북조선이었고, 내가
상대하던 사람들은 남한이 아니라 중국인들이었다고.
대체 왜 누명을 쒸우려 한 걸까? 뭔가 잘못 된거 아냐?
경애하는 지도자 김정일 동지의 어머니를 연기한 난
일호배우였다고. 북조선에 아무 잘못도 하지 않았어.
하지만 결국 나는 저 멀리 중국 본토로 도망쳐야 했어.
거기서 기다리고, 또 기다렸지. 하지만 남편한테서
집으로 돌아오라는 연락은 끝까지 오지 않더군.
(비트) 그 사람 이름을 가르쳐 줄 수야 있지만, 아마
벌써 처형 당했을거야...

처음 미국에 왔을 때 난 매일매일 아침드라마만 봤어.
<가이딩 라이트>, <제너럴 호스피탈>. 누구를
사랑할지 본인이 선택하고, 누구와 결혼할지 스스로
선택한다는 개념. 난 당신이 좋아, 난 그를 사랑해.
"나, 나, 나." 우리란 개념은 없고 전부 *나*뿐이더군.
그래서 내 전 남편, 프랭크 화이트에게 드라마에서
배운걸 써 봤더니, 그게 먹히더라구! 물론, 내가 그와

결혼한 건 미국 시민권을 얻기 위한 거였지만, 어쨌든 우리는 아이도 가졌고, 그럭저럭 결혼생활을 같이 잘 해 나갔지.

(비트) 아주 똑똑한 아이지, 내 딸 미나 말이야. 똑부러지고, 명랑하고. 겨우 열 두 살인데 벌써 나만큼이나 키도 크다고. 우리 딸 아무 것도 몰라. 그 애를 어디로 데려갔는지 당신 정말 몰라?

당신 한 번도 사랑 해 본적 없지. 그렇지, 박 요원? 그래, 어쩌면 사랑이라는 게 당신한테는 어려울지도 모르겠어. 남자 같은 버릇, 헝클어진 커트머리에 저음의 목소리. 그 이상한 남부엑센트며. 남자들은 그런 걸 좋아하지 않지. 당신네 FBI 동료들이 쬐끔한 동양인 여자가 백인 남자처럼 행동한다고 정말로 당신을 더 진지하게 대해주나? 다코타 요원은 내가 우아하고 여성스럽게 행동했기 때문네 날 믿고 동등하게 대해준 거라고. 당신, 외모에 좀 신경 쓰셔야겠어.

내가 그를 순전히 이용한 거라고 생각하고 있는것 같은데, 다코타 요원과 나는 진심으로 서로를 사랑했고, 서로를 깊이 이해하고 있었어. 난 그에게 진짜 유용한 남과 북한에 대한 정보통이었고, 나에게 그는 연인이자 친구였지. 내가 북한쪽을 만나고 돌아오는 길에 붙잡힌 것 때문에 나를 간첩 혐의로 기소하는 거라면, 그건 흉칙한 계략이라고, 박 요원. 내가 이쪽에 정보를 주려면 북조선에도 무언가 줘야 한다는 사실은 누구보다 당신이 잘 알고 있잖아? 그게 세상의 이치야, 오는 게 있으면 가는 것도 있는 거라고. 지난 10년 동안 당신들 조직이 사용한 지도는 다 내가 갔다준 거라고. 그게 다 어디서 나타난 거라고 생각해?

그리고 이제 와서 갑자기 나더러 배신자라고?
살인용의자? 절대 아니지. 내 생각을 말해 줄까? 난
너무 많은 걸 알고, 조직에서 제일 힘있는 남자의
마음을 훔친 죄로 위협받고 있는 거라구.
그래, 내가 송 동지에게 몇 월, 몇 일, 몇 시에, 무슨 핵
지도를 어떻게 줬는지 말해줄 수 있어. 하지만 내가
배신자라는 건 절대 인정할 수 없어. 이렇게 될 줄
몰랐던 나 자신을 탓할 수밖에. 전에도 누명을
썼었는데 여기서 또 쓰지 말라는 법이 있나? 여기
미국은 자유의 땅이기 때문에?

(비트) 도망쳐 나와 몽골 사막에서 지냈던 밤들,
추위는 뼛속까지 스며들고 심장은 으그러질 것만
같았어. 고요하고, 적막하고, 황량하고, 별들은 수없이
반짝였지. 거기서 끝냈어야 했는데. 그래, 거기서.
희망이라는 건 참 위험한 거야. 마음 속 헛된 상상은
아주 위험하지. 난 알아. 굶어 죽어가는 인민들에게
'강성대국의 꿈'을 위해 정진하라고 환상을 심어주는
짓을 배우 노릇하며 했으니까. 우린 남한에 대한
거짓말 속에서 자랐어. 남한 사람들이 굶주려 흙이나
먹고 있다고? 고층빌딩은 햇빛에 반짝이고
슈퍼마켓은 먹을게 가득한데? 중국에서 TV로 본
남한의 모습이 늘 나를 괴롭혔지.

북조선에서 나를 쫓았던 이유가 바로 그걸거야. 이
모든 걸 보았고, 알고, 자각하고 있으니까... 박 요원,
난 '너무 많은 것을 안다는 이유'로 계속해서 신에게
벌 받고 있어. 그게 정말 죈가? 당신도 조심하는 게
좋을 거야. 당신. 나와 다를 바가 없으니까.

캐서린, 북한 선전가요인 "적기가"를 흥얼거리기
시작한다. 의자를 돌리며 박 요원으로 분한다.

105

장면 10: 박 요원 / FBI 취조실

박 요원: *(선전가요의 마지막 후렴구를 마무리하며)*
그 북한 노래, 이렇게 부르는게 맞나? 당신 정말...
시적 표현력이 풍부한데. 하지만 곁다리는 치우고
본론으로 돌아가자고. 당신은 북한을 탈출해서,
북한에 맞서서 남한을 위해 일했지. 그런 후 남한과
미국의 정보원으로 일했고. 그리고 다시 당신을
엿먹인 북한에게 남한과 미국을 팔아 넘겨? 그러고선
오히려 당신이 억울하게 붙잡혔고, 당신이 미국 국방
기밀을 팔아 넘긴 게 실제로는 우리 미국쪽을
도우려고 한 거였다. 그걸 나보고 믿으라고? 내 참...

(신경이 거슬려) 니가 사랑에 대해서 날 가르치려해?
당신은 스파이짓을 위해서 딸을 앞잡이로 이용했고,
연인과 남편을 소모품처럼 갈아치운 여자야. 똑똑히
알아둬. 내 어머니는 나를 위해 모든 걸 포기했어.
교수로서의 경력, 삶, 그 모든 것을. 그리고 내
어머니는 절대 나를 위험에 처하게 두지 않아. 진짜
사랑이 뭔지 제대로 이해하고 있는 사람이 있다면,
그건 바로 나라고. 정신차리고 일어나시지.

박 요원, 머리를 흔들면서 미나로 분한다.

장면 11: 미나 / 독방

독방에 갇힌 미나, 우리에 갇힌 동물처럼 서성인다.
미나, 자신에게 속삭인다.

미나: 일어나. 일어나, 정신차리고. *(소리친다)*
일어나라구요, 엄마! 벌써 오후 1 시야, 심심하다구!
시차 땜에 피곤한 건 아는데...나랑 여름방학 때는 더 많이 놀아준다고 했잖아.

미나, 의자에 안으며 가상의 캐서린과 대화한다.

엄마, 이번에는 어디 갔었어? 과테말라? 마카오?
이번에도 사진 안 찍었어? 왜 엄만 사진을 안 찍어?
내가 인터넷으로 사준 디카 잘 안 돼? 그니까, 그 사진
같은 건 내 컴퓨터로 일초면 인터넷에 올릴 수 있는데.
완전 껌이야. 세상에, 엄만 "투 따우전드 앤 레잇,
아임 소 쓰리 따우전드 앤 에잇 (2000 and late, I'm
so 3008 엄만 구석기 2000년대, 난 3008년 시대)*".
블랙아이스피슨데, 엄만 이 노래 모르지? (혹은:
세상에, 엄마는 가끔 보면 구십년대 구석기
시대라니까.)

응, 엄마가 지난 주에 외국 간 사이에 아빠가 왔다
갔어. 바둑도 두고 놀았는데 내가 완전 이겨버렸지,
재미있었어. 근데 아빠 엄청 우울해 보이더라구.
그래서 또 구구절절 얘기 늘어놓는 거 다~ 들어줬어.
엄마가 많이 보고 싶은가봐. 엄마랑 아빠랑 처음 만난
날. 아빠는 그날 엄마가 뭐 입고 있었는지 완전 다
기억한다. 핑크색 드레스에 질끈 묶은 검은 생머리.
아, 근데 이번에는 엄마가 '엄청 아리따리'하다는
새로운 표현을 쓰더라구. 아빤 엄마만 생각하면 되게
감상적이 되나봐.

(비트) 나도 엄마처럼 예뻤으면 좋겠다. 알아, 알아,
내가 특별하단 거. 동양과 서양, 음양의 조화로 태어난
새천년의 히트상품. 엄마 뱃속에서 나온 깜짝 선물...
하지만 난 예쁘지도 않고, 엄마랑 닮지도 않았잖아.

---

* Black Eyed Peas 의 "Boom Boom Pow"에 나오는 가사. 자신이 가장
앞서있고 다른이(랩퍼)들은 시대에 뒤쳐졌다는 뜻.

(일어서며) 다들 내가 남미 출신 히스패닉이라고 생각한다구, 엄마! 아무도 날 귀여운 동양 여자애라고 생각 안 해. 내 눈이랑 머리 색깔이 이렇게 더러워 보이는 갈색이니까. 엄마 피부는 엄청 부드럽고 털도 하나도 없는데 난 시커먼 털이 온 몸에 숭숭 나 있잖아. 거기다가 엄마는 주근깨도 없고. 이 주근깨? 하나도 안 귀여워. 무슨 똥싼 자국 같다구. 어떡하면 난 엄마 아빠를 이렇게 안 닮을 수가 있지? 그니까, 아빠가 뭐 그렇게 잘생긴 건 아니지만 암튼 눈은 푸른색이잖아. 난 무슨 잘못 섞은 케익 반죽 같아.

미나 다시 의자에 앉는다.

뭐? 신성스런 유기적 창조품? 그런 말은 또 어디서 들었어? 정말 그렇게 생각해? 그냥 예쁘다는 말보다 훨씬 쿨하다. 그리고 생각해보니깐, 난 엄마보다 눈도 크고 속눈썹도 길잖아. 그니깐...내가 엄마보다 쪼끔 더 예쁘다고도 할 수 있지.

미나, 마치 그녀의 엄마가 만지듯 두 손으로 얼굴을 감싼다. 일어나서 한동안 멀리 응시한다.

엄마, 빨리 와서 구해주세요...

미나, 일어나서 의자 뒤로 가 가디건를 걸치며 박 여사로 분한다.

장면 12: 박 여사 / 거실

박 여사: 우리 말썽꾸러기 지영이. 어릴 때 매일 싸우고 다녔어요. 하튼, 왈가닥, 완전 터프 톰보이. *(싸우는 시늉을 한다)* 그렇다고 깡패 같은 짓을 하고

다닌 건 아니구요. 아시잖아요, 남부 조지아주 작은 마을에서 혼자 동양애로 크는 게 쉽지 않다는 걸.

지금도 기억이 납니다. 어느 날 오후 지영이가 집에 돌아왔는데, 얼굴은 온통 얻어맞은 자국에, 치마는 찢기고, 코에서는 코피가 나고. "지영아! 이게 무슨 일이야? 어떻게 된 거니!" 소릴 질렀더니 지영이는 날 그냥 쳐다보기만 하더라구요. 그리고선 그냥 '못된 녀석들' 좀 손봐줬다고.

그러더니 욕실로 걸어가서 가위를 집어 드는거에요, 글쎄. 난 지영이가 무슨 끔찍한 일이라도 저지를까봐 무서워서 얼른 달려가 가위를 뺏으려고 했는데, 어찌나 지영이가 벌써 커버렸던지. 그리곤 날 보더니 이렇게 말하지 않겠어요. "엄마, 걱정 마. 그냥 머리 자를려고." "그러지마, 지금 머리가 얼마나 예쁘고 기니. 지영아, 하지마." 하튼, 내 말 안 듣지, 이 녀석.

그러더니 싹둑, 싹둑, 그 길고 예쁜 머리칼을 잘라버렸어요. 그리곤 거울을 한참이나 응시하더군요. 내가 거기 서 있는 것 조차 까맣게 잊어버렸나봐. 머리를 좀 다듬어주려고 등 뒤로 다가서니까 깜짝 놀라 펄쩍 뛰더라고요. 내가 그랬죠, "그래, 니가 맞고 엄마가 틀렸다. 부처님께서 머리카락은 무지의 잡초라고 하셨어. 그래서 스님들이 대머리잖아. 넌 그렇게 치렁치렁 쓸데없이 긴 머리를 하고 다니기엔 너무 똑똑하지. 그래, 이 새로운 헤어스타일 마음에 든다."

아휴, 물론 언짢았죠. 그렇게 예쁜 내 딸이 갑자기 피터팬놈 처럼 변해버리다니. 하지만 전 지영이의 그런 행동을 일종의 의식으로 인정해주고 싶었어요. 그리고 지영이에게 약속했죠. "엄마도 앞으로 흰머리가 나더라도 염색하거나 뽑지 않을게. 나이가 들면서 인생의 무상함을 알고 겸손해질 수 있도록. 알았지?" 우리는 손가락을 걸고 약속했어요. 그리고 엄지도장.

박 여사, 새끼 손가락으로 약속하고 엄지 손가락을 찍는다.

하지만 그게 내가 할 수 있는 전부였어요, 약속이나 하는것. 내가 딸을 늘 지켜줄 수 없고 그 아이가 누릴 수 있는 것들을 모두 해 주지 못한게 너무 슬펐어요. 하지만 하도 일하느라 항상 피곤해 있었죠. 명성있는 교수에서 이주 노동자가 됐으니.
(의자에 앉는다) 아무튼, 내가 염색을 하지 않는 이유는 바로 그거에요. 알지, 염색하면 15 년은 젊게 보일거라는 거. 하지만 지영이랑 약속을 지켜야 하니까요.

박 여사, 가디건를 의자에 올려놓고 박 요원으로 분한다.

장면 13: 박 요원 / FBI 취조실

캐서린과 어린 미나가 함께 찍은 사진이 뒷벽에 비춰진다. 박 요원, 책상 위 파일에서 이 사진을 집어 든다.

박 요원: 당신 딸 미나와 함께 미국에서 찍은 이 사진, 이게 몇 번째 얼굴이지? 다섯번짼가? 지금 얼굴은 여기 미국에서 했나? 아니면 서울에서? 한국 성형외과 의사들 솜씨가 세계 제일이라고들 하던데.

박 요원, 사진을 들고 의자를 천천히 앞으로 밀어 '거울' 앞에 선다.

당신 예쁜 얼굴이 그립지 않나? 아침에 일어나서
거울을 보면 내가 누굴까 하고 혼란스럽진 않고? 당신
딸이 당신 얼굴을 닮지 않아서 신경 쓰이지 않나?
*박 요원, 캐서린의 얼굴을 만지듯 손을 뻗히며 즉시
의자에 앉아 캐서린으로 분한다. 사진은 여전히 손에
들려있다.*

장면 14: 캐서린과 박 요원 / FBI 취조실

캐서린: *(박 요원의 손을 치듯)* 얼굴에 손대지 마! 내
얘기를 마저 듣고, 그 잘난 FBI 파일에 기록해서
승진하고 싶으면 다신 내 얼굴에 손대지 마.

손에 들고 있는 사진을 보며.

그래. 이 사진은 미나가 다섯 살 때 LA 에서 찍은
거야. 이봐, 박 요원. 모든 걸 말해주지. 원한다면
세세하게 내가 분석 요약 정리까지 다 해줄 수 있어.
하지만 그 전에 나와 내 딸을 보호해주겠다고
약속해야돼.

긴 비트.

좋아. 대한민국 국가정보원... 그쪽 훈련은 식은죽
먹기였지. 셰익스피어 연극도 하루면 다 외우는
사람이 남한 사람인 척 하는 건 쉽지. 난 다섯 달 만에
완벽한 남한 사람이 됐지. 미국식 영어, 중국어,
일본어, 러시아어, 독일어도 배웠고. *(독일어로)* 두
하스트 다스 아우크 게탄, 오더?* (너도 배웠지?)

---

* Du hast dass auch getan, oder? 혹은: 당신도 훈련소에서 다 배우지 않았나?
  Du auch hast dass an der akademie gelernt, oder?

난 내가 아는 북조선에 대한 모든 정보를 해석하고
해독해서 국정원에 넘겼지. 하지만 대부분은 그 바보
같은 선전영화에 나온 내용들이었으니까, 진짠지
아닌지 알게 뭐람. 그래도 국정원에서는 내가 정보를
줄 때마다 엄청나게 들떴어. 그들에겐 내가 이래적인
최고의 정보통이었던 거지. 그래서, 난 다시 고위급
관리로 존경을 받을 수 있었고.

"아, 자아도취에 빠진 불쌍한 여배우 같으니, 관심
받고 싶었구나." 아니, 그 이상이었지. 북조선은 날
쓸모 없고 위험한 인물로 간주했어. 그 병신 같은
아들놈이 아버지가 만들어 놓은 체제에 위협을
느끼니까 내 존재 자체를 말살해 버렸다고. 내가 왜
남한 최고의 정보원이 되어야 했는지 이제
이해하겠어? 내가 실존한다는 걸 확인하기
위한거였다고.

왜 나약한 인간은 존재감 같은 것에 집착하는 걸까?
사람은 언젠가 때가 되면 그냥 왔다가 가는 건데
말이야. 훗, 이 삶, 다 환상이고 터무니없는 거라고.
잔인한 농담이지. 거기에 덧붙여 인간은 또 '자만심'
이라고 불리는 걸 가졌고. 그게 모든 걸 엉망으로 망쳐
버리지. *(소리 내어 웃는다)* 당신 나한테 정말
고마워해야돼. 난 지금 당신한테 사랑, 삶, 진짜
여성스럽게 꾸미는 법 등에 대해서 공짜로 가르쳐주고
있으니까. 게다가 검은 나비 프로젝트에 대한 모든
것도. 제발, 그러니까, 당신도 내 딸 미나가 어디
있는지, 그 애한테 무슨 짓을 했는지 알려줘야 공평한
것 아냐?

*캐서린, 의자에서 일어나 사진을 책상에 놓으며 박
요원으로 분한다.*

박 요원: 정말 뛰어난 배우시군, 그 과장된 말씨 하며... 하지만 아직 구체적인 내용은 하나도 말해주지 않았잖아. 송 동지라는 작자에게 건네준 미국 핵 지도가 어느 것인지, 그걸 다코타 요원에게서 어떻게 훔쳤는지, 그리고 대체 그런 짓을 왜 했는지!

그러니까, 옆길로 새지 말라고. 당신 딸은 무사해. 지금 독방에서 우리가 잘 돌봐주고 있어. 물론, 보장된건 아무것도 없지만.

박 요원, 의자 왼편으로 다가간다.

거봐, 사전에 이런걸 다 생각해 놓고 일을 벌렸어야지. 이기적으로 자기 생각만 말고. 그 엿 같은 철학 같은 거 가르치려 들지 말고. 자, 당신이 남한에 그렇게 중요한 존재였다면 왜 미국을 위해서 일하기로 한 거지?

박 요원, 의자에 앉으며 캐서린으로 분한다.

캐서린, 자신 왼쪽에 있던 박 요원에게 말한다. 시선은 박 요원이 맞은 편에 앉는 것 처럼 그 동선을 천천히 따라간다.

캐서린: 내가 선택한 게 아니야! 남한에서 날 FBI 에 팔아 남긴 거라고. 그래야 북한과 미국, 전세계에 대한 정보를 쉽게 얻을 수 있으니까. 내가 하겠다고 한 건 아무것도 없어. 두쪽 다 합작해서 내 경력을 꾸며내고, 신분증을 위조하고, 기록을 조작해서 미국 대학원 학위까지 받아 낼 수 있도록 계획을 세웠지. 전부 사실이야.

이봐, 당신이 내 입장이라면 어떻게 했을까? 몽골에서 자살했을까? 남한으로 도망쳐서 거기에 머물렀을까?

113

미국 정보원으로 일 했을까? 아니면, 모두를 배신하고 전의 삶을 망친 나라에 자신을 팔아 넘기겠다는 의심을 받을까?

말했지, 당신도 나와 다를 게 없다고. 아마 그래서 당신이 나에 대해 그렇게 불안해하고 신경이 날카로와 있는걸꺼야. 이 모든 일이 시작됐을 때 나에겐 아무런 계획도 없었어. 내 운명은 내가 김정일 어머니를 닮은 예쁜 얼굴로 난 죄 밖에 없다고. 그게 나에게 배정된 팔자였지. 그 후로 내가 선택한 거라곤 죽지 않고 살아남기로 한 것뿐이야, 알겠어?

캐서린, 박 요원의 의자에 앉는다.

박 요원: 운명? 동양인들이 매일 대는 핑계, 그 엿 같은 팔자타령! 보라고. 북한을 탈출하기로 선택한 것도 당신이고, 정보원으로 팔려가는 선택을 한 것도 당신이고, 당신 삶을 망쳐버리는 선택을 한 것도 본인이라고.

(일어서며) 내 생각은 말야. 당신 아주 한이 맺혔어. 또 자만심으로 가득하지. 자만심, 당신이랑 당신 딸이 아주 즐겨 쓰는 그 말. 네 인생을 망쳐버린 북한이 오히려 너를 필요로 하도록 만들고 싶었던 거야. 그래서 뭐든지 팔아 넘길 준비가 되어 있었고, 당신 딸까지도. 당신의 그 잘난 그...'이고'라는 말로는 표현이 부족해, 당신의 그 잘난...'존재의 흡족감'이란 걸 채우기 위해서 말이야. *(캐서린을 노려본다)* 내 말이 틀렸나? *(천천히 의자에 앉는다)*

박 요원, 캐서린의 의자에 앉는다.

캐서린: 날 뭐라고 불러도 좋아. 스파이, 삼중간첩, 정체성 혼란에 빠진 여배우. 하지만 감히 내 딸에게

상처를 준다는 말로 나를 모욕하지는 마. 정말이지 계획 된 건 아무것도 없었다고. 그게 바로 가장 기가막히게 불행한 점이지.

캐서린, 고통스러워하며 가슴을 움켜쥔다. 아니, 박 요원인지도 모른다. 신음소리와 함께 가슴에 박힌 화살을 뽑아내는 미나로 분한다.

장면 15: 미나 / 독방

미나, 가슴에 박힌 화살을 뽑으며.

미나: 그니깐 내가 심장에 맞은 화살을 뽑은 다음에, 또 다른 그리스 비극을 연기했어. 오이디푸스 컴플렉스. 그 제목은 뭔 뜻인지 모르겠는데, 내가 쓴 인용 문구는 완전 짱이야.

미나, 대사를 읊으며 연기한다.

"폭군- 힘만 무지하게 센 또라이가 폭군이란 뜻이야. 폭군은 자만심의 아이. 그 구역질 나는 컵에서 무모함과 허영을 가득 떠서 마신다네. 저 높은 꼭대기에서 재만 남은 희망없는 구렁텅이로 곤두박질 칠 때까지."[*]

누가 동양 여자애는 표현력이 부족하다고 그랬지?

유치장의 알람이 울린다. 미나, 귀를 틀어막고 구석에 가서 숨는다.
피자가...오는 거면 좋겠는데.

---

[*] 연극 "오이디푸스 콤플렉스"의 대사

문으로 다가가 구멍을 통해 밖을 엿본다.

말했잖아요, 울 엄마가 스파인지 뭔지는 난 아무것도
모른다구요! 만약에 아는게 있어도 절대로 말
안해줄꺼야! 배고프다구! 밥 좀 달라구요!

또라이 새끼!

미나, 책상으로 걸어가며 즉시 박 요원으로 분한다.
책상위 파일안에서 종이 한장을 꺼내든다.

장면 16: 박 요원 / FBI 취조실

박 요원: 당신을 다음 범죄 혐의로 기소한다.

아랫글 영상 비춰짐.

미 연방법 제 371 장; 소득세를 확인, 산출, 사정 및
징수함에 있어 국세청의 적법한 정부 기능을 지연,
방해, 저해 및 무효화시킬 목적으로 미합중국을
침해하고 사취할 것을 모의하는 행위. 그리고 미
연방법 제 794 장; 외국 정부를 원조하기 위해 국가
방위 정보를 불법적으로 인도하는 행위.

의자 뒤로 걸어간다.

우리가 당신을 귀화시키고, 고용하고, 당신을 믿은 건
당신이 오로지 미국 정보원으로만 일할거라는
전제하였어. 서울의 그 비싼 호텔에서 호의호식하면서
즐기게 해 준 것도 전부 북한 원자로에 대한 정보를
확인하고, 영변에서 대체 무슨 일이 벌어지고 있는지,

그 빌어먹을 우라늄은 어떻게 됐는지 알아내라는
거였다고, Mrs. 화이트. 그래서 내 부모님과 같은
이민자들이 낸 피 같은 세금을 자그마치 오백만
달러나 당신에게 쏟은 거라고. 근데 당신이 11 년
동안 그 돈을 다 날려먹고 우릴 장난감 처럼 갖고
놀아?

박 요원, 의자를 돌려 캐서린을 마주본다.

(나지막이) 쟤들이 뭐라고 하는지 알아? "어쭈,
예쁘장하고, 여리여리한 동양년이 우릴 갖고 완전
놀았났네? 와, 누가 상상이나 했겠어?" 당신이 한
짓이 나 같은 사람들한테 무슨 영향을 끼치는지나
알아? 내가 승진을 거듭해도, 여기서 아무리 오래
일한다고 해도, 내 어머니께서 단체 개발 위원회
따위에 고생해서 기부한다고 해도, 우리 동양인들은
고맙게도 너 같은 얼 빠진 놈들 덕분에 항상 의심의
눈초리를 받는다고. 미국 남부, 그것도 불교 집안에서,
아무도 제대로 발음 못하는 지영이란 이름을 갖고
자란 내가 너무 빤히 아는 사실이지. 나같은 사람이 널
추적해서 잡은게 천만 다행이다. 당신이 몸 팔아 꼬실
수 있는 병신 같은 백인남자가 아니라. 당신 담당
다코타 요원, 아니지, 죽은 FBI 요원 다코타처럼. 진짜
현대판 마타하리로군. 누가 당신 얘기 영화로
찍어야겠는데.

(비트) 당신 같은 사람 요즘 어떻게 하는지 아나? 911
이후, 잠재적 테러리스트를 도우려는 배신자가 된
정보원을?

당신 배울 만큼 배웠고, 여러 나라 말을 하는데다
철학을 나불대는 삼중간첩이니까 "하마티아"라는

단어의 뜻 정도는 알고 있겠지? 몰라? 부끄러운 줄 알라고. 당신 딸은 공부해서 숙제까지 냈는데. "과녁을 놓치다"라는 뜻이지. 모든 걸 이룬 잘난 영웅이 너무 자만심이 넘쳐, 바로 그 실수 때문에 지옥의 나락으로 떨어지는 거지.

이러다가 당신 딸 죽이겠어. 잘 생각해봐.*

박 요원, 책상으로 걸어가 가디건을 집어 들고 박 여사로 분한다.

장면 17: 박 여사 / 거실

박 여사, 관객들을 둘러보며 손으로 그녀의 얼굴을 따라 동그라미를 그린다.

박 여사: 음, 인상이 아주 좋으시네. 그쪽도. *(또 다시 동그라미를 그린다)* 아실지 모르겠는데 한국 사람들은 얼굴을 읽지요. 관,상,학. 뭐, 우스꽝스러운 부분이 좀 있기는해요. *(관객을 가르키며)* "당신은 뒤통수가 납작하지 않고 짱구형이니까 똑똑한 사람." 아니면, *(또 다른 관객을 가리키며)* "당신은 귀가 부처님처럼 기니까 회사에 큰 도움이 될 얼굴상." 아니면 "당신은 아주 예쁘지만 여우처럼 생겨서 남편 잡아먹을 얼굴상." 이렇게 말이 안되게 단순한 점이 있습니다. 하지만 말이죠, 우리가 살아온 날들이 우리 얼굴에 드러나는 건 사실입니다.
내 얼굴을 보세요. 주름 하나 없이 깨끗하잖아요?
(이마가 보이도록 머리를 뒤로 넘긴다) 이마에 주름이

---

* 원작 연극에서 이 두 문장은 박요원이 처음이자 마지막으로 한국말을 하는 부분이다. 이후 상사와 문제 제기의 발생 요인.

없다니까요! 이건 내가 얼굴을 찡그리지 않고
살아왔다는 얘기죠. 난 66 년* 동안 별로 얼굴을
찡그려본 적이 없어요. 하지만 오늘, 얼굴을 찡그리게
됐습니다. 왜냐? 존 유 같은 사람이 있기 때문이에. 그
사람 얼굴을 보니까 목에 살집이 덕지덕지 살 붙어서
말이야, 아주 게걸스럽게 생겼더라구요. 북한의
뚱뚱한 지도자처럼 생겼어요. 그렇게 생긴 사람은
절대로 믿으면 안 돼요. 그 사람이 한국계라니...
아이구 창피해, 정말.

아니, 존 유가 누군지 몰라요? 이봐요, 뉴스를 좀
봐야지, 뉴스를. 그 애국자법에 대한 메모를 써서
논란을 일으킨데다가 부시 정권 때 합법적 고문을
옹호한 변호사잖아요. 그 사람 말로는, 미국이 제네바
협약을 지킬 필요가 없다는 거에요. 세상에,
아부그라브 교도소에서 고문당한 사람들 다 봐 놓고도
어떻게 그런 말을 할 수가 있는 거지? 그래서 내가
인터넷에서 찾아놓는게 여기있는데...

박 여사, 책상위 파일속에서 메모를 찾는다.

어디갔나... 아, 여기 있네요.

아랫글 영상 비춰짐.

제네바 협약. "비전투원, 무기를 내려놓은 전투원,
부상, 구금 또는 기타의 어떠한 이유로든 전투에
참여하지 않은 전투원은 어떠한 경우에도 인도적
대우를 받아야 하며, 특히 인간의 존엄에 반하는 폭력,
굴욕적이고 모멸적인 대우를 금지한다. 특히 여성은

---

* 공연 연도에 따라 나이 조정 가능

강간, 강요된 매춘 또는 모든 형태의 성적 추행을
비롯하여 그 명예를 훼손하는 어떠한 행위로부터도
보호받아야 한다."

인터넷! 하지만 사람들은, "존 유는 말야, 하버드대학
나와서 예일 졸업하고, 워싱턴에서 일도 하고, 책도
썼고... 어쩌고 저쩌고, 그렇니까 믿을만하지." 이렇게
잘못 생각하죠. 아마 그 사람 부모님은 자기 아들을
아주 자랑스러워할거에요. 하지만 사실은
부끄러워해야 돼요. 그 사람들도 나같은 6 25 전쟁
세대잖아요. 그런 알만한 분들이 어떻게 자식을
그렇게 키울 수가 있죠? 나 같으면 그런 자식은 당장
호적에서 파버리겠어요. 의절이라는 건 그럴 때 하는
거라구요, 여러분 자식이 흑인이랑 결혼했을 때가
아니라! 하인스 워드를 보세요, 얼마나 대단해, 슈퍼볼
MVP!

존 유가 버클리대학에서 교수라구? 하! 그런 사람이
교수가 아니지, 나 같은 사람이 진짜 교수지. 그
사람... 그 사람은... 테러리스트라구! 젊은이 의식과
인간권리에 대한 테러! 내 딸이 그 자식을 감옥에
처넣었으면 좋겠어요!

(숨을 고르며) 아이고, 진정해야지. 그런 바보같은
사람 때문에 심장마비가 오거나 주름이 생기면 절대
안 되니까.

박 여사, 책상쪽으로 걸어간다. 가디건을 접어 책상에
놓고 박 요원으로 분한다. 박 요원, 책상에 놓여진
메모를 보며 잠시 멈춘다. 놀라며 책상 바깥쪽으로
급하게 돌아나와 무대 앞쪽 중앙으로 이동한다.

장면 18: 박 요원 / FBI 사무실

박 요원: *(흥분한 목소리로)* CIA 가 그 여자를 이송해 나갔다니요, 과장님? 대체 어디로 데려간 겁니까? 이 사건은 제 담당이란 말입니다. 뭐, 온몸에 자살 폭탄이라도 둘러 즉각적으로 위협이 되는 인물이 아니라구요!

과장님, 아시잖아요. 제가 지금까지 아홉 달 동안 한숨도 못 자고 이 건을 혼자서 맡아왔다는거, 잘 아시잖아요. 코피터지도록 노력해서 송동무에 대한 모든정보와 거래 날짜들, 그 여자가 언제, 어디서, 뭘 했는지, 누구랑 잤는지, 누구랑 연애를 했는지 다 알아내고 있는 중이라구요. 다코타 요원의 죽음을 끝까지 파헤치려면 아직 그 여자가 필요해요. 우리 요원이 죽었습니다 과장님. 그건 CIA 소관이 아닙니다! 이놈들, 도데체 뭔 소릴하는건지. 우리가 범인을 잡아야 할것 아닙니까. 하루만 더 주시면 보고해 드릴 수 있습니다. 그냥 손 놓고 CIA 에 넘기라구요? 제가 만든 자료를 갖고 뭘 어떻게 해야 할지도 몰라요, 그 자식들은. 그 여자한테 불리한 쪽으로 써먹기나 하겠죠.
제가 그 여자와 너무 가까워졌다니요? 제 담당 아닙니까, 제 사건요. 대체 무슨 말씀을 하시는 겁니까?

(비트) 취조에서 한국어를 사용한건 의도적이고 계산적인 전략이었습니다! 아니요, 그 여자의 편을 들거나 공감해서도 아니고 정신을 못차려서도 아니였습니다. 취조동안 무슨말이 오갔는지는 보고서 안에 번역된 기록에 다 설명해 놓았습니다 과장님! 여기 보시면...

긴 침묵.

제가 믿을수 없다고... 누가... 그랬습니까?

박요원 침착을 잃지 않으려 애쓴다.

과장님, CIA 가 그 여자를 미국 땅에서 빼내 해외
수용소로 보내버리면 다시는 우리쪽으로 돌아오지
못할 거라는 걸 누구보다 잘 아시잖습니까.

그 딸은 어쩌구요? 캐서린 화이트를 어디로
데려갔는지 모르십니까? 우리가 이렇게 놓아버리면...
세상에...

박 요원, 충격에 휩싸인채 의자로 걸어가 주저앉는다.
두손으로 머리를 감싸며.

젠장...
어떻게 이런일이...

박 요원, 의자를 무대 윗쪽으로 돌리며 캐서리으로
분한다.

인터루드 (막간극) /구천 혹은 연옥 세계

*캐서린, FBI 취조실에서 태국 수용소 감옥방으로
옮겨진다.*

*비디오 영상, 또는 무대 보조원이 정체 불명의
'고문자'역을 연기하는 방법, 혹은 원작에서와 같이
간단한 의자의 회전을 동반한 극적인 조명등으로 표현
될 수가 있다.*

장면 19: 캐서린 / 태국의 수용소

*캐서린, 손이 등 뒤로 묶여져 있다. 고문을 당한
흔적이 역력하다. 한국 민중가요 "아침이슬"을 부르며
의자를 돌려 앉으며 발을 질질 끈다. 서서히 의식을
차리면서 외국 고문자를 발견한다.*

캐서린[*]:
(한국어로)
여기요! 여기가 어디죠?

(일본어로)
니홍고 와까리 마스까? (일본어를 하십니까?)
에이젠또 바끄와 도꼬데스까? (박 요원은 어디 있죠?)

(중국어로)
니 회이 쇼우 쫑웬마? (중국어를 하십니까?)

---

[*] (일본어) 日本語が分かりますか？ エージェント　パークはどこですか？
(중국어) 你會說中文嗎？

어떻게 이런 일이... 나한테 약속했다고... 박 요원 어디갔어! 비겁한 년... 그 여자가 약속했다고! 나랑 내 딸을 도와주겠다고 약속했다고. 그 여자한테 모든 걸 다 털어놨어, 다. 다, 당신은 뭐가 뭔지 아무것도 모르잖아...

잘못했어요. 제 딸이 어떻게 됐는지만 말해줘요, 그럼 모든 걸 다시 털어놓을게요. 약속해요. 하라는 대로 뭐든지 할게요.

좋아, 좋아. 계속 이런 식으로 나오면 나도 아무 말 안 할거야. 나보다 더 많은 걸 알고 있는 사람은 이 세상에 없다는 거 몰라?

긴 침묵. 캐서린, 주위를 둘러보고 방 안에 악취가 나는 것을 맡는다.

"여기 아직도 피 냄새가 남았구나. 온갖 아라비아 향수로도 이 작은 손을 향기롭게 만들진 못하리라."*

아주 엄청난 캐릭터야, 레이디 맥베스. 모두가 그렇게 얘기들했지. 근데 난 사실 이 지경이되어서야 이해가 되네.

"자, 이제 침대에 들자. 누군가 문을 두드리고 있구나. 자, 자, 자, 미나야, 손을 이리 주렴. 이미 끝난 일은 돌이킬 수 없단다. 이제 침대에 들자."* 미나야, 엄마가 잘못했다, 엄마가 잘못했어...

---

* 셰익스피어 <맥베스>에 나오는 대사.
* 셰익스피어 <맥베스>에 나오는 대사를 변형한 것.

고문자가 캐서린에게 가까이 다가온다.

아, 안돼... 제발...제발...

장면 20: 캐서린과 박 여사 / 구천 혹은 연옥 세계

캐서린이 채이고, 얻어맞고, 고문당하는 모습이 슬로모션으로 보인다.

캐서린, 의자에 빙글빙글 돌아간다.

그리고는 의자에서 떨어져 나와 바닥에 무릎을 꿇는다. 그리고 몸이 서서히 널부러진다.

긴 침묵이 흐른 후, 손이 움직이기 시작하면서 기도하는 자세를 취한다.

캐서린이 천천히 일어나면서 무릎을 꿇고 불교와 기독교식 기도를 드리는 박 여사로 분한다.

박 여사: 나무아미타불 관세음보살.
주 예수의 이름으로 기도드렸나이다.

박 여사, 일어나 의자에서 가디건을 집어들어 어깨에 걸친다.

장면 21: 박 여사 / 거실

박 여사: 지영이가 이런 걸 한 번도 본적이 없어요.
정신 나간 사람 꼴을 해서는 집에 들어오는데, 어디
지옥에라도 다녀온 것 같더라니까요. "지영아, 무슨
일이니?"라고 물어봐도 아무 말도 안하고. 눈은
횡하게 비어있더라구요. 그래서 더 자세히
들여다보니까 아주 어두운 슬픔이... 예전에 이런 눈을
본 적이 있습니다.

난 6.25 전쟁 때 얘기하는 걸 별로 좋아하지 않아요.
지영이는 어렸을 때 늘 어땠냐고 캐물었죠. 조지아
대학 가서는 동양계 미국인, 아시아 유산 문화 등에
대한 수업을 전부 다 들었죠. 몇 월, 몇 일, 몇 시에
무슨 일이 어디서 어떻게 일어났는지 줄줄이 꿸
정도가 됐지만, 책을 읽었다고 전쟁을 겪는 게 어떤
건지 진짜 알 수는 없는 법이죠.

(비트) 내가 어렸을 때 우리 가족은 인천에 살았어요.
네, 네, 그 새 국제공항이 있는 도시. 아주
나이스하죠? 맥아더 장군, (똑똑한 영어 발음으로)
매~가~서 장군이 유명 또는 악명 높은
인천상륙작전을 펼친 아주아주 중요한 항구 도시죠.
인천상륙작전. 1950 년, 구월 십오일. 난 그 때 겨우
네 살이었죠. 그 당시 인천은 커다란 동물원과
유원지가 있는 걸로도 유명했어요. 그래서 한국전쟁에
대한 제 첫 번째 기억은 아주 흥미진진했습니다. 마치
눈 앞에서 노아의 방주와 서커스를 동시에 보는 것
처럼. 부둣가에 엄마와 함께 서서 이마~만큼 큰 배에
동물을 싣는걸 쳐다보던 기억이 나요.

이렇~게 큰 기린, 엄~청 큰 코끼리, 원숭이, 양, 개,
늑대, 우리, 우리에 담긴 여러 동물들. 어머니한테
소리쳤죠. "엄마, 엄마! 저것 좀 봐! 진짜 희한하다.
진짜 신난다! " 근데 어머니께서 아주 공허한
눈빛으로 절 바라보시던 걸 기억해요. 난 너무 어려서
그걸 이해못하고 어머니 눈이 이상하게 멍하게
비었다고 생각했는데, 사실 그건 아주 슬픈
눈빛이었어요. 아주 적막하고. 아주 어두운. 그리고
엄마는 내 손을 아주 꼭 잡았어요.

그 당시 이승만 대통령이 미국과 동맹을 맺었으니
아마도 그건 미국 배였을거라고 추측되지만 그 배가
어디로 갔는지는 아무도 모르죠. 근데 어떻게 배에다
한국 사람들보다 동물을 먼저 피난시키냐구요. 그
다음 생각나는 건 찜차 뒤에 앉아서 부산으로 피난
내려가는 거구요. 이게 6.25 에 대한 내 첫 번째
기억입니다.

난 한 번도 지영이에 대해 걱정을 해본 적이 없어요.
하지만, 이번에 그 눈, 우리 어머니를 닮은 그 눈빛을
보고 나니 너무 걱정이 되서 지영이 방에 들어가 그
북한 스파이에 대한 파일을 들여다봤어요.

그 스파이의 어린 딸이 화살을 쏘는 시늉을 한다는
점을 아주 눈여겨 읽었어요. 수사관도, 의사들도 그
애가 뭘 하는지 모르고 있다고 적혀있는데 내 생각에
그 애는 아마 기마족 흉내를 내고 있는 거라고
생각합니다. 한국, 그러니까 코리아라는 단어는 옛날
만주까지 뻗어 몽고에 닿아있던 고구려라는 나라에서
유래한 거랍니다. 기마족은 징기스칸 사람들과 비슷한
거죠. 용감한 한국의 기마 전사. 그 어린 아이는
엄마가 해 준 한국 신화 애기를 들은 게 분명해요.

그 스파이가 뭔가 끔찍한 일을 저질렀다는 건 알아요. 하지만 그 사람들이 그 어린애까지 심문하는 건 아주아주 잘못된 겁니다. 파일을 보니까 그 애한테 약을 먹여 환각을 보기 시작한다던데...

박 여사, 가디건을 책상에 올려놓고 미나로 분한다.

장면 22: 미나의 전쟁 / 독방, 박 요원 / FBI 사무실

미나, 쿵쿵 걸어오다 의자에 앉는다. 변덕스럽게 의자를 돌린다.

미나: 멍청이, 또라이! 상상 속 친구랑 엄마한테 얘기 좀 했다고 내가 미쳤다구? 그럼 이 거지 같은 곳에서 나 혼자 뭘 하고 있으란 말야? 내가 뭐 울 엄마에 대한 정보라도 너희들한테 흘릴까봐? 울 엄마 스파이 아냐! 동양인이 여러 나라 말을 한다고 해서 다 스파이는 아니라구! 너희들 정신 나간것 아냐?

미나, 의자를 책상쪽으로 옮기며 박 요원으로 분한다.

박 요원: 제가 지금 정신이 나가서 사표 쓴것 아닙니다, 과장님. 상부에서 제 보고서를 전부 조사하고, 내 나라가 제 충성심을 의심하는데 제가 뭘 어떻게 더 이상 일을 할 수 있겠습니까? 그렇습니다, 저는 캐서린 화이트와 그 딸이 당한 일들에 동의하지 않습니다.

박 요원, 의자를 책상으로부터 멀리 밀며 다시 미나로 돌아간다.

미나: 우리 집에 너희들이 쳐들어와서, 자고 있던
엄마랑 날 끌어내구서. 엄만 내 손을 잡고 안 놓으려고
발버둥치고... 그리고선 날 이 거지 같은 감옥에
쳐넣고, 약이나 먹으라고 하면서...내가 미쳤...???

미나, 멀리서 들려오는 전투 북소리에 귀를 기울인다.
의자에서 천천히 일어나 의자등을 앞을 향해 돌리고는
말 위에 오르듯 다리를 걸쳐 의자에 앉는다. 가상의
'말'인 의자를 밀어타기 시작하면서 화살을 쏘기
시작한다.

내가 누군지 몰라? 저 사람들, 진짜 적들을 내가 쏴서
없앨거야. 무자비한 폭군에 맞서 싸우는 난 용감한
전사. 구역질 나는 컵으로 무모함과 허영과 자만심과
하마티아를 가득 떠서 마시는 피에 굶주린 독재자,
내가 널 없앨거라구! 퓽~!

미나, 북소리가 계속 커짐에 따라 지평선을 훑으며 수
많은 적들이 그녀를 향해 다가오는 것을 본다.

저기 적들이 온다...

미나, 의자 뒤에 숨었다가 함성을 지른다. 숨을 크게
들이쉬고 의자 뒤에서 뛰쳐 나와 마지막 남은 화살을
쏠 준비를 한다.

장면 23: 박 요원 / 구천 혹은 연옥 세계

박 요원, 미국의 어머니에게 국제전화를 건다. 전화기
너머로 녹음된 태국 안내원의 목소리가 흘러나온다.

태국어 안내음: 텔레 타이 국제 전화카드를 이용해서
주셔서 감사합니다. 여덟짜리 핀 넘버를 입력하고
우물 정자를 누르십시오. 즉시 연결해 드리겠습니다.*

박 요원, 책상 쪽으로 천천히 다가간다. 조명이 바뀌는
동안 시적 무용의 제스처 (피나 바우쉬같은). 그리고
가디건을 집어 들고 박 여사로 분한다.

장면 24: 박 여사 / 거실

박 여사:

그리하여 화살은 날아가고.
깊고, 어두운, 시간의 허공 속으로.

내 아이야, 너는 어디로 가고 있느냐?
적들이 아직 너를 따라 쫓느냐?

지평선을 향해 질주하는 너,
결코 숨길 수 없는 그 역마살 때문에.

화살촉은 결국 상처를 내는구나.
흉터는 남고, 피는 굳는다.
마음은 닳아가고 영혼은 지쳐가네.

---

*코어 콥 쿤 티 챠이 버 리 칸 바뜨 토 라 숩 라 황 쁘라테트 텔레 타이 차 니드 텀
느겐. 카루나 코드 마이 렉 핀 페아드 래아그 탐 두에이 크롱 마이 시 리얌. 랄 자
탐 칸 첨 토어 칸 토 콩 쿤 나이 마이 차르.

(태국어) ขอขอบคุณที่ใช้บริการบัตรโทรศัพท์ระหว่างประเทศ Tele Thai
ชนิดเติมเงิน กรุณากดหมายเลข PIN 8 หลัก
ตามด้วยเครื่องหมายสี่เหลี่ยม เราจะทำการเชื่อมต่อการโทรของคุณในไม่ช้า

너는 결국 과녁을 꿰뚫어 황소를 죽일 것.
하지만 아이야,
죽음 뒤에 네가 할 수 있는 일은 무엇이냐?

지영이가 태국에서 건 전화를 받고 그 북한 스파이
사건에 대해서 쓴 시입니다. 지영이는 지금 외국
수용소들을 뒤지면서 그 스파이를 찾고 있습니다.
나한테는 청소년 정신병원 같은 데서 그 딸아이를
찾아달라고 했는데, 전화 연결상태가 별로 안 좋아서
전부 다 알아듣지는 못했어요.

참으로 이상한 때입니다. 괴상한 일들이 일어나는. 난
우리 가족이 미국에 도착했을 때 이런 잔인하고
부조리한 시간들은 끝났다고 생각했어요. 난 미국이란
나라를 사랑한답니다. 우리가족을 지켜줬고, 또
우리에게 많은 걸 준 곳입니다. 그래서 난 이런
생가하면 너무 무섭고 가슴 아픕니다. 다른 이민자
가족들, 그러니까 우리들 바로 옆집에 살고 있는
이웃사람들이 실제로 무슨 일을 하고 사는지 모르고
있다가, 순식간에 사라져 버리는 경우. 전에 있던 삶이
한 순간에 사라지는 일들이 일어 날때 말입니다.

아무튼, 벌써 시간이 이렇게 늦었네요. 무거운 얘기를
너무 많이해서 미안하네요. 이 늙은이를 찾아주셔서
정말로 고맙게 생각해요. 여러분은 참 조용하고 내
말도 유심히 잘 들어주고, 참 인상이 좋아요. 난
여러분 얼굴이 좋아요. 지영이가 얼른 돌아와 다음
번에는 여러분도 지영이를 만나실 수 있으면
좋겠어요.

박 여사, 사람들에게 가라고 손짓한다.

그래, 들어가라, 들어가.

박 여사 무대를 떠나려다 마지막으로 뒤를 돌아본다.

집에 조심해서 들어가세요.

끝